THE LOST ANGEL

E5

ROSECRADDICK

RUTH SABERTON

CW01654759

Copyright © 2022 by Ruth Saberton

All characters, organisations and events in this publication, other than those clearly in the public domain, are fictitious and any resemblance to real persons, living or dead, is purely coincidental.

The opinions expressed in this book are solely the opinions of the author and do not represent the opinions or thoughts of the publisher. The author has represented and warranted full ownership and / or legal right to publish all materials in this book.

The moral right of the author has been asserted.

All rights reserved. No part of this publication may be reproduced, stored in a retrieval system or transmitted, in any form or by any means, without the prior permission of the publisher, except for the use of brief quotations in a book review.

Created with Vellum

FOR SALE

Sea Angel **PENMARLOE • ROSECRADDICK • CORNWALL**

For sale for the first time in eight years, an exciting refurbishment or redevelopment opportunity in a prime coastal location. Situated in a breathtaking south-facing waterfront position with panoramic views over Penmarloe Harbour and out to sea.

Ground Floor

Lounge • Dining room • Kitchen • Utility/boot room

First Floor

Three bedrooms • Family bathroom

Single Garage (on Sea Lane)

Second Floor

A large attic, currently a studio but with potential for a master suite or self-contained letting unit

In all about 1.5 acres

Approx. Gross Internal Floor Area 1868 sq. ft

Rosecraddick 4.7 miles • Fowey 14 miles (All distances are approximate)

Sea Angel – for sale freehold

Sea Angel is situated in a spectacular waterfront position perched above the popular seaside village of Penmarloe. The property faces south and offers a superb opportunity for renovation and refurbishment.

The house, built around 1931, is encircled by stone walls and sits within a private and spacious garden. There is also an extensive kitchen garden with raised vegetable beds and a large attic studio. A rear gate leads onto a footpath giving pedestrian access into the village.

The property lies adjacent to the South West Coast Path, in an area of outstanding natural beauty, and is close to the village of Penmarloe, one of Cornwall's most spectacular and unspoilt waterfront locations. It is believed that the original owner of the property fought in the First World War with the renowned Cornish war poet Kit Rivers.

Viewings

Strictly by appointment with the selling agent

PROLOGUE

Before

1914

British Lines and No Man's Land

THEY'D SAID it would be over by Christmas but they were wrong.

Dawn broke over the Western Front on Christmas Eve and its pale light turned the wintry world into a magical landscape sugared with hoar frost and frozen iron-hard, just as in all the ancient carols. Although the sun climbed bravely into a bright blue sky and sparkled on the pockmarked landscape below, the men hunkered down in their trenches had no time to admire the scene or to remark upon its festive appearance. For them, Christmas was from another time where there were no shells and bombs and screams. It belonged to a lost world that had taken on the semblance of a dream.

The day dragged itself onwards until the sun began his

slow slither back into the mud, and the soldiers burrowed in the mire braced themselves for the next round of shelling to buck the earth and rip the biting air. Blowing on numb fingers and drawing on cigarettes from their Christmas issue gift tins, their hearts were as heavy as the clay clagging their sodden boots, and they ached for home. Some wrote letters to their wives or sweethearts. A few scratched lines of poetry into notebooks. Others snatched fragments of sleep and dreamed of goose and plum pie instead of bully beef and whatever mean scraps they'd managed to beg and barter from local farms and villagers. Their breath rose like plumes of incense at Midnight Mass and mingled with their desperate prayers that this war would soon be over and each man safely home to hold his loved ones close.

As the night chased the day away and scattered stars across a deep indigo sky, the soldiers realised to their surprise that the enemy guns had ceased grumbling and the world was abruptly still. The men held their breath, unnerved and confused. Was the enemy planning a surprise ambush? Were they even now, on this most holy of nights, priming their weapons and mustering the ranks for an assault? What was happening across the battle-scarred wastes of No Man's Land and behind enemy lines? What new horrors were creeping closer with the lengthening shadows?

Braced for an attack, the soldiers abandoned the letters they were writing and tucked cherished photographs inside their jackets. Weapons primed and nerves as tight as violin strings, they sat waiting for the onslaught that must surely come – but when eleven o'clock arrived without incident, they were puzzled. Some men wanted to venture over the parapet to see what the enemy were up to, but others were convinced this odd stillness was a cunning trick to lure them to their end – Christmas or not.

"Or maybe they don't want to fight tonight? Christmas is holy to all men," one soldier suggested. He was carving as he spoke, and shavings drifted into the mud earth like woody snow. "Maybe they don't want to fight when we should all be in church?"

"Fritz keeps Christmas too, don't he?" agreed one, and the others nodded slowly.

"Silent night," said the woodcarver quietly. He drew a small carved angel from the breast pocket of his jacket and traced her wooden face with his forefinger. "Holy night. Remember?"

And it was then, as though the woodcarver's words had magicked them into existence, that the opening notes of a Christmas carol floated over the iced landscape. The haunting tune was played on a cornet and was soon accompanied by voices. Although the words were sung in a foreign tongue this was a carol so dear and so familiar that it tightened knots in every throat and made eyes prickle with homesick tears.

"*Stille Nacht, heilige Nacht*," carolled the voices from across No Man's Land. "*Alles schläft; einsam wacht.*"

In the Allied trenches the men listened, unable to believe what they were hearing.

"It's Fritz! He's bloody singing!"

"He's singing Christmas carols!"

One by one the men followed their wary officers out of the trenches and ventured over the parapet. The woodcarver was the last of them, and his index finger caressed his carved angel's wooden face as tenderly as though touching the cheek of his sweetheart. When he joined his comrades his eyes widened, for although the midnight sky blazed with stars and a bright moon poured light over the shell-bruised earth, brighter still were the candles set on makeshift Christmas trees erected along the tops of the opposite ramparts, and the happiness ringing in the accented voices calling out festive greetings.

"A very Merry Christmas to you, English soldiers! Merry Christmas, Tommy!"

The British officers, afraid of treachery and tricks, ordered their men to be silent. Yet as the singing and festive greetings continued to ring out across No Man's Land the soldiers found it impossible to resist joining in. Before long, answering greetings rang up and down the line, and if nervous hands still rested on rifles laughter and carols from both sides filled the cold air.

Not a single shot was fired that night and when the clouds drifted over and light snow began to fall, each flake seemed a blessing drifting down from Heaven as a balm for torn earth and tired hearts. It was Christmas! The holiest and the most wondrous time of the year, when the world paused to worship the Christ Child and even men at war with one another could find peace. Eventually the carols and calls of celebration faded away and the men returned to their quarters, but their hearts were lighter and that night their sleep was peaceful. The woodcarver's hand rested on the smooth face of his angel and for once his dreams were not of blood and bone and death but of the sweetness of his true love's face and the wonder of her smile.

When the sun rose the next day the world, with a light dusting of snow, sparkled like a Christmas card. Birds, silenced for so long by artillery, filled the air with swelling song and filled hearts with joy. Soldiers on both sides lay down their weapons and marvelled at this rare bright glimmer of hope during a war already overlong and ugly. From the bleakness of the conflict's tight grasp of misery dawned a new Christmas story to offer, for a few hours at least, light in a world that had seemed relentlessly dark and joyless.

Calling to one another, the soldiers clambered out of their bunks and, clutching gifts of cigarettes and food, stepped from their trenches and dugouts into No Man's Land and legend.

1

The Present
London
Ellen Shaw

WHEN HAD Christmas stopped being a time of year she loved, Ellen wondered. Was it possible to pinpoint the moment when the magic of glittering window displays and fairy light festooned trees had faded? When had December, once characterised by an agonising wait to open the advent calendar's final window, ceased to be the slowest month of the year? And why did the opening bars of 'Last Christmas' now make her feel panic rather than a flutter of festive excitement?

There must be something wrong with her. Everyone loved Christmas.

Was this lack of festive cheer because she had split up with Steve? Being single was always harder at Christmas, when every advertisement seemed to feature cute couples unwrapping gifts in their tartan pyjamas or strolling hand in hand through some Dickensian high street. The party invites were all for Ellen Shaw plus one, which highlighted his absence neatly, and it was harder to escape the mistletoe-sprig-waving office sleaze when there wasn't a ring on your finger. But Ellen didn't think it was being single that had stolen her Christmas spirit. Although she missed Steve it had been a mutual parting of the ways and the right thing to do. Their relationship hadn't been a grand passion but rather a high school friendship that had stretched a little too far into adult life. Was it wrong to want more? To hold out for a love that lit up the world and made even the greyest day sparkle?

Her grandmother hadn't thought so. Clara North had been a huge romantic, loving Grandpa Harry for over half a century, and it was the glimpses she'd caught of their love that made Ellen believe there must be more. Though old, the way the two smiled at one another suggested a whole secret language, and they'd always held hands. When Grandpa Harry became so ill, Clara's patience and tenderness had been pure love distilled, and when he died Ellen knew Clara missed him dreadfully. But how many people found that kind of love? It belonged to films and novels, not the 21st century. What if true love was consigned to the past alongside steam trains and tea dances – if it had ever existed at all?

"The right one for you is out there," Clara had promised whenever Ellen expressed doubts. "You'll know him when you find him, love, because it feels like coming home. Never settle for less than that."

Ellen, trusting Clara's wisdom, had taken this on board, but sometimes it was hard to keep the faith that true love existed. It was harder than ever since her grandmother had died. Ellen missed Clara terribly and as she worked her way through emptying out her grandmother's under-stairs cupboard, a cobweb-strewn and musty cave crammed with the treasures of a lifetime that had any meaning for their owner alone, she blinked away tears. No matter how much Ellen reminded herself that Clara had enjoyed a full and happy life, living well into her late nineties and passing away peacefully at home, surrounded by the family who loved her so dearly, her heart refused to be soothed. Her friends were sympathetic and kind, but there was a general assumption that because Clara had been so old there was little reason to be sad, because old people died, didn't they? It was the way of things. The natural order. Grandparents went first because they'd had their turn. A good innings. Life went on.

Ellen abandoned her sorting and sat back on her heels to dab her eyes with her sleeve. The familiar ache of loss still gnawed at her heart although she knew logically that her friends had made valid points. She feared she had even uttered them herself in the past as a well-intentioned way of offering comfort, but it was hard to accept them now that they were applied to Clara. Her grandmother might have been old but she had been the linchpin of the family, and Ellen would miss her wise words and calm presence more than she could ever say.

It was also hard to be sanguine about Clara's passing when the bulk of preparing the family home for sale had fallen to Ellen and her mother, Maggie. For months they had sifted through the flotsam and jetsam of over nine decades, spending hours agonising over what to keep and what to sell or give away. Clara hadn't been a huge fan of decluttering or downsizing. She'd watched Marie Kondo with a perplexed expression and, turning to Ellen who'd been visiting at the time, wondered what one did if *everything* 'sparked joy'? If everything was a treasure and had a story all of its own, how did you ever choose what to reject and what to keep?

Judging by the rooms crammed with books and trinkets, the wardrobes full of clothes dating back to the nineteen-fifties and even that small understairs cupboard packed tightly with everything from dustbags for vacuum cleaners not owned for decades to long-widowed gumboots and shoes, Clara's solution had been to keep everything. It had all meant something to her, Ellen concluded, and every item had been precious. From the battered doll's pram with one wheel missing to the paint-splattered trench coat Grandpa Harry had always donned when decorating, everything here was a treasure. Consigning most of this hoard to the skip felt like a betrayal.

"Pick a few things to remember her by," Maggie had suggested. Maybe you could choose a piece of jewellery, like Daniel did?"

Ellen's big brother had asked for Clara's engagement ring, a request which prompted lots of excited speculation that he was gearing up to propose to his girlfriend, Siân. Ellen quietly picked a brooch which she recalled Clara had loved, but as much as she would cherish this piece she knew it was not in this particular item that her grandmother's memory lived on within her. Neither was it in photographs or trinkets, but rather it would be at Christmas that she would always think of her grandmother. Granny Clara *was* Christmas! She had adored the season and always made it special, so being without her this year was going to be very hard. It was because of this rather than her breakup with Steve that Ellen was struggling to find her festive mojo. She felt as though there was little to celebrate this year.

Clara North had been born Clara Schneider, and she

had grown up enjoying her parents' German festive traditions. Later on, when she had her own daughter, Maggie, she wove these customs into her family's Christmas celebrations and these had been celebrated ever since. For Ellen and her brother as children and beyond, Christmas Eve was the most magical and exciting time of the whole season, for in Germany this was when gifts were exchanged – which meant no long wait until Christmas morning! The extended family gathered at Clara and Harry's house, where the air was heavy with the scents of stollen and gingerbread and, with their fingers and faces sticky from sugared almonds, the children would decorate the tree, something keenly anticipated since it was never put up until they had all gathered together. The candles were always lit after carols were sung, and then the presents were exchanged and the cakes enjoyed. Ellen would tumble into a camp bed clutching her new toys to her chest, and with a full tummy. She would drift away to the sweet notes of 'Silent Night' and the low laughter and chat of the grownups downstairs. The years passed and Ellen and Dan grew up, but the family still kept Christmas Granny Clara's way, except for fairy lights on the tree instead of candles. Ellen supposed that without Clara's steady presence, and the alchemy of her wonderful baking, things were bound to change. It was the way of things.

But it was very, *very* unsettling.

Life had to move on, Ellen reminded herself as she turned her attention back to dragging out the boxes wedged at the back of the cupboard. Granny Clara would have been the first to remind her of that. Danny would propose to Siân and in time they would make their own family and establish their own Christmas traditions. There would be new arrivals and new traditions. This was how things were meant to be, even if it felt hard to bear.

"You need to have some fun," Maggie had concluded earlier on when they were driving across Harrow to drop several bags off at the charity shop. "You've had a tough year, love. You've had a breakup and a new job, and helped me nurse Granny. She wouldn't want you to hide away and be sad."

"I'm not hiding away," Ellen protested, although this was exactly what she was doing and she was definitely sad. After a hard year helping her mother nurse Granny Clara, twelve months in which she'd in effect put her social life on hold in order to spend nights at Clara's house to ensure she was able to stay at home right until the very end, Ellen wasn't in the mood to socialise or look for love. Her heart was far too heavy.

"You're young and you should be having fun, Elly. When did you last go on a date?" Maggie pressed. "You need to get out there again. Steve did!"

Ellen rolled her eyes. Maggie was quoting Anna, a friend of Ellen's, who had an annoying habit of finding single men who would be *just perfect* for her and urging her to get 'out there' and over her ex.

"Steve wasn't nursing his grandmother," she pointed put. "Steve wasn't clearing her house either. Or trying to run a freelance editing business. Anyway, I'm glad he's happy."

The point was that Ellen had had no desire to start dating while Clara was so sick and the family were busy working out a rota for who could care for her. And now, heavy-hearted and with a social calendar visited only by tumbleweed, she still hadn't any energy left for dating. Unless she met somebody whose smile felt like a homecoming and just the mere glimpse of whom was enough to make her heart soar, what was the point? She certainly had no desire to be trawling the wine bars and clubs with Anna. If this was what was meant by being 'out there', Ellen was very happy to be sorting through cupboards and up to her neck in dust and junk.

"I'm fine, Mum. Stop worrying."

But Maggie wasn't prepared to give up. "I'm your mum. It's my job to worry. Granny was worried too. She was always hoping you would meet somebody nice. That was what she wanted for you more than anything, love. She was so very happy with my dad – they were soulmates, and she would've loved nothing more than to know you'd met yours."

Clara Schneider and Harry North's romance was the stuff of family legend. During her final weeks, Clara had retold their story frequently and with a faraway expression in her eyes. Ellen loved to listen to these tales, and as her grandmother talked she knew that Clara became the girl she'd been all those years ago when Grandpa Harry, the dashing Army medic, brought her to England as his bride. It was the 1950s and, she'd explained, they'd encountered all kinds of prejudice because she was German, but nothing mattered apart from their love for one another. Although Harry had died a decade ago, Ellen knew her grandmother had missed him every moment of every day that had followed. Clara's last word was her husband's name, and she had smiled as she'd whispered it, looking far beyond the room to a place Ellen couldn't see. She hoped Harry had come to meet her, young and handsome once more as he held out his hand to his beautiful young bride. True love like that was rare. Maybe it didn't even exist any more? Ellen had certainly never found anything to compare to it, and she was starting to think she never would.

"Not everyone can have what she and Grandpa had."

"Why not?" asked her mother sternly. "It wouldn't hurt not to give up entirely, my girl. Granny always said there's was somebody special waiting for you. She was quite funny about it towards the end, wasn't she? Borderline obsessed, I'd even say."

Ellen smiled; Clara had said this over and over again. She had also been convinced that crossing over would grant her special powers to 'sort her family out'. Nobody dared argue with her; Clara was such a force of nature that it had seemed quite possible, and Ellen often felt as though her grandmother wasn't far away at all, but just in her kitchen baking something delicious as always while listening to the afternoon play on the radio.

"I know there's somebody special for you, Ellen love," Clara would always insist, in the tone of voice none of the family had to dared argue with. "He'll be your angel, mark my words. I'll send you a sign. Make sure you look out for it."

Ellen always laughed but Clara was serious. "You wait! Once I'm up there with Grandpa Harry, I'll be on the case. I'll send your perfect match over. You see if I don't. Keep your eyes peeled for the sign!"

But no sign had arrived, and the heaven-sent Prince Charming had failed to materialise. Ellen was starting to lose faith in fairy tales. Her sweet grandparents had been lucky to exist in a more innocent age, before the advent of Tinder and Naked Attraction. The romance they'd enjoyed was well and truly absent nowadays. There was no magic in the swiping which had replaced the tea dances and the stolen moonlit kisses. Ellen thought the world was a sadder place for it too.

"And I'm happy as I am," she said staunchly. "Can you please stop going on about it?"

Maggie Shaw knew when to drop the subject. The determined tone of her daughter's voice was pure Clara, as were her auburn curls and amber eyes. The serious nature was her grandfather's, she thought. Schoolteacher Heinrich had been an earnest and thoughtful man, and, like the great-granddaughter he had never met, he had felt things deeply.

"How about we take an hour out to do our Christmas shopping once we've dropped this lot off?" Maggie suggested, hoping to lighten the mood. "There's a festive market in the mall. We could even have some mulled wine and a mince pie if you like?"

But Ellen couldn't face the full-on festive onslaught of Christmas. One note of 'Silent Night' and she'd crumble. "I'd rather get the clearing finished. Then we can enjoy Christmas properly," she said.

And so here Ellen was now, regretting this choice a little as she crawled into the narrowest space in the house, her hands getting covered in grime and cobwebs lacing her hair. Fat spiders scuttled away, disgruntled by such a rude disturbance, and Ellen sympathised. They were probably happy here in the dusty peace. Nobody liked being forced to go out and about!

Spiders and flickering silverfish aside, the understair cupboard was almost empty now. Ellen dragged out a heavy toolbox followed by the skeletal remains of an old Silver Cross pram. Tucking loose strands of her coppery hair back beneath her headband, she crawled back into the cupboard, into the pinch point where the stair treads met the hallway, to drag the final box out. Once this was free all she had to do was sweep up the dust and another task would be complete. Soon Granny Clara's house would be empty, the For Sale board would go up in the garden, and it would be as though none of these items, and the people who'd once treasured them, had ever lived here. Although all the familiar sounds would be heard by a new family, the smell of the Sunday roasts summoning her and Danny in from playing in the garden would be only memories, and even the old apple tree in the garden might make way for a deck. Everything was changing.

One box left. One cardboard box which dammed the flood tide of the future. Ellen wiggled the box in an attempt to dislodge it, but it refused to budge and feeling frustrated, she tugged at the edges. The decades-old cardboard, fragile and a little damp, disintegrated beneath her fingertips and its contents spilled out in a colourful waterfall.

"Oh!"

Whatever Ellen had been expecting to find – old electric plugs, perhaps, or more coils of the wire Grandpa Harry had insisted putting away just in case – it wasn't tinsel, baubles and old-fashioned glass fairy lights. The last box had contained a long-forgotten selection of Christmas decorations, tatty and tired and certainly not up to modern electrical standards.

Ellen delved into the unexpected treasure trove, and loops of gummed paperchain, creased and fragile with age, whispered against her skin. The contents must have been decades old, for there were no elegant hand-carved pieces or Murano glass here. In fact there were no decorations of the kind Granny Clara had collected over the years to adorn her beautiful tree. Neither was there a glittering star to crown it, but rather a jaunty homemade affair fashioned from coat hanger wire covered with balding silver tinsel. More tinsel in garish shades of peacock blue, gold and pillarbox red spewed like innards from the remains of the box, and plastic baubles rolled across the floor, decades out of fashion and brittle with age. Ellen suspected her grandfather had shoved the box under the stairs long ago, where it had remained ever since, forgotten and unloved. It seemed a shame that the things that must have once created that tingle of Christmas magic were now tatty and only fit for the dustbin. Had her mother made the star as a child? And ought she to keep it?

There's no point in being sentimental, Ellen told herself firmly as she reached for a black bin liner. Granny Clara couldn't have seen these decorations for years, so they certainly weren't heirlooms. She scooped up handfuls of tinsel and paperchains and stuffed them into the bag. The baubles followed and then several strands of fairy lights, clipped together with dark brown twists of wire ending with old style two-pronged plugs. Soon all that remained was a bundle of cloth tied up with a ribbon, green with age and mould-spotted. Intrigued, Ellen unwrapped it and discovered a carved angel nestled inside.

This was different, for unlike the rest of the box's contents, this decoration was beautiful and somehow timeless. The angel's wooden face, with her sweetly curved lips and prayerfully closed eyes, was serene, and as Ellen traced the smooth curve of the angel's cheek with her forefinger she marvelled at the delicate way the waterfall of wooden hair framing the heart-shaped face almost seemed to move. Whoever made this had been wonderfully talented.

"Why are you hidden there?" she asked.

But the angel, of course, said nothing and simply smiled to herself. She was going to keep her secrets.

Keen to examine her find more closely, Ellen crawled backwards into the hall where late afternoon sun buttered the parquet floor. The warm light turned the angel's face to honey, and the small ornament seemed to glow with a life all of her own. She was only about seven inches tall, but somebody had taken the time to carve her with loving detail and fashion her a robe from what looked like hessian. At some point somebody had made a crude attempt to paint the hair and face, but their handiwork was flaking now and echoes of the original features were re-appearing in patches like the landscape when mist lifts. Ellen turned the angel around and around in her hands, drawn to this simple decoration although she couldn't articulate why. Something about it made her heart feel lighter than it had for a long time.

It felt peaceful and familiar.

"Good Lord! I haven't seen that for years! It's the lost angel!" Maggie, halfway down the stairs, had paused in mid-descent. Her face was a study in surprise.

"You've seen it before?"

"Oh yes! She used to be on the top of the tree at my grandparents' house. How strange to see her after all this time! It feels like it was only yesterday that Grandpa Heinrich lifted me up to pop her on the top. Where on earth did you find her? She's been missing for years."

"In a box of old decorations under the stairs."

"My parents must have put that there after they cleared my grandparents' place. Goodness, how Mum moaned about the junk they kept! Isn't it funny how things come around? I'll do my best not to do that to you and Dan."

"I'll hold you to that," laughed Ellen.

Maggie took the angel in her hands, stroking the wooden face wonderingly.

"I seem to remember Mum was hunting high and low for this at one point. We thought it must have been thrown out in the move, and Mum was so upset. She said the angel had meant a great deal to her father. She felt terrible about losing it."

"So it's old." Ellen wasn't surprised, since the lost angel was worn smooth with age and possessed a simple purity that ornate modern pieces, with their sparkle and glitter, lacked. How many Christmases had this angel seen? What would she be able to tell them if she could speak?

"If she belonged to Grandpa Heinrich she must be a least a hundred years old," said Maggie. "Don't get your hopes up that she's worth anything, though. She's homemade and very tatty now, poor old thing."

Ellen felt affronted on the angel's behalf. "I think she's beautiful."

Her mother smiled wistfully. "You're right. She is, and I loved her as a child. Funny how we forget. It always felt like Christmas once the angel was up on the tree. Do you know I even tried to give her a makeover once with some enamel paint! Grandad Heinrich went mad."

"You did this paint job?"

"I'm afraid so. I was in big trouble for that. Grandpa said he'd had her since the war and she hadn't survived the trenches to be ruined by me. He didn't get cross very often, but he was really angry that day."

Ellen scraped the angel's wooded tresses with her fingernail. Flakes of paint drifted to the parquet.

"I think the paint will come off fairly easily. I could have a go at cleaning her up if you don't want her."

Something about the angel resonated with Ellen. Maybe it was the purity of her face or the obvious care in every stroke of the blade that had carved her sweet smile. Or even knowing that this simple decoration had witnessed over one hundred Christmases come and go, and been placed on top of the tree by Granny Clara all those years ago when she was a little girl living in Hamburg.

"You can have her, love, but I don't think she's anything special. Her value's purely sentimental," her mother said.

But Ellen disagreed. To her the lost angel was something very special indeed, and she was already looking forward to cleaning her up. Who knew what lay beneath the thick paint and years of dirt?

"Your grandfather loved her, though," she pointed out. "She was special to him."

"True,' agreed Maggie. "I wish I could remember why. Sabine – do you remember her? She's my second cousin, because her grandmother was Grandpa Heinrich's sister – might know more. I'll drop her a line when I get a minute."

Ellen slipped the angel into her bag. It made no sense, but she couldn't have been more certain that the angel was meant to go home with her than if Grandma Clara was standing at her side, nodding her approval and talking about signs.

Ellen had been meant to find the angel.

2

December 1913
Penmarloe, Cornwall
Jack

It was so bitterly cold during Midnight Mass that even the stained-glass saints in the windows seemed to shiver, but Jack Tregenna didn't notice. Oblivious to the blue tip of his nose and the way his breath huffed in little clouds as he uttered the familiar responses and joined in with the ancient carols, all he could think about was the beautiful girl sitting several pews in front of him. Although she was only a matter of some feet away, it might as well have been a hundred miles, but Jack would have sat willingly in the icy church for a year if it meant catching even a fleeting glimpse of her. He would trudge barefoot through the Arctic if this meant he could be in the same place as Caroline Sweethouse. Loving her from afar was painful, but not being able to see her at all?

The notion was unbearable.

Jack slid his hand into his jacket and his fingers caressed the smooth wood of the carving carried deep within his pocket. It had been carved with love, every delicate whisk of his blade a gesture of devotion, and he could hardly wait to give it to Caro. It was, Jack thought with a glow of satisfaction, the finest piece he had ever created, and as exquisite as the girl upon whom its face was modelled. As just a humble carpenter, Jack might not be able to present Caro with exotic hothouse blooms and diamonds, but she possessed an entire florist's shop's worth of carved peonies, roses and orchids fashioned by his own hand and polished smooth from hours of sanding. Each second was a labour of love, for every bloom was a true symbol of his feelings for Caro. She was his muse, his angel, his everything – and when Jack was with her all obstacles melted away because they were meant to be together.

Jack hadn't intended to fall in love with a girl whose rank was set so far above him. Who would willingly seek out a love that swelled in your breast like the rising tide only to drown you in an undertow of deep despair? Intellectually, it was easy to list all the reasons why loving Caro Sweethouse was a foolish notion, but the heart wants what the heart wants, and Jack's heart was set on the Rector's beautiful daughter. Ever since he had first laid eyes on Caro, golden hair streaming in the wind and white skirts billowing as she scrambled down the cliff path, he'd been unable to put her from his mind, and she blazed before his vision like the dazzling imprint of the sun on closed eyelids. Jack knew that this would never change. He would love Caroline Sweethouse until the day he died. There would never be another girl for him.

Jack had met Caro by chance on a golden summer's evening. After a long day toiling in the carpenter's shop he was walking down to the cove for a swim. He was looking forward to plunging into the cold sea and striking out for the horizon. Swimming was the closest Jack came to freedom now. His father had died the summer before, leaving Jack to care for his mother and sisters and shoulder the responsibility of the family carpentry business. Jack sometimes wished he could keep swimming and leave behind all the burdens that were his. How would it feel to discover the world which lay beyond the confines of the village and the dusty workshop? To walk away from Jack Tregenna, the village carpenter, and towards the man he could become? Jack was afraid he would never know that man now. He would never abandon his mother and the girls, for they were his family and even though he was just seventeen he was now the man of the house and the provider. What did his own dreams matter when he had such responsibilities? His life was laid out before him and it was as unmovable as the granite quay and jagged rocks beyond; Jack Tregenna was Penmarloe's master carpenter just as generations of Tregenna men had been before him. It was his destiny.

But how he secretly wished that his destiny could have been different. If only he was free to choose. If only the stars had been set differently and if only his father hadn't caught the fever which ended his life far too soon. Life was full of *if onlys*, and Jack thought they were the saddest words in the world. He much preferred the *what ifs* with their wealth of possibilities and hope.

Before Saul Tregenna had died, Jack's heart had been set on becoming a sculptor rather than a carpenter. Whenever his hands caressed the rough edges of a piece of new-hewn wood the spirit of the finished piece concealed beneath the grain and knots whispered its secrets, and before Jack even picked up his chisel an enchanted alchemy was already at work. When he wasn't busy with one of the mundane jobs his father had assigned him with, Jack was always to be found whittling as his clever hands coaxed a squirrel from a chunk of ash or spurred a horse into full gallop from a leftover piece of walnut. He hadn't questioned the idea that he would eventually take Saul's place in the workshop and spend the rest of his days in Penmarloe until the day when the new schoolmaster showed his pupils pictures of Michelangelo's work. As Jack gazed at photographs of marble creations that were so lifelike they seemed almost to breathe, something deep inside him had stirred. How he longed to create something timeless and wonderful like the David or the Pietà! How must it feel to create works of art that moved men to tears and spoke of timeless truths, and which would exist long after their creator was forgotten? In a heartbeat Jack Tregenna knew his dearest wish was that his work could transcend tables and cabinets. He wanted to sculpt, and for his work to lift the hearts of all who saw it. The enthusiastic young schoolmaster had ignited the small spark of ambition which soon flared into a furnace of longing.

"You have a rare talent, Jack!" he had exclaimed when Jack showed him some of his carvings. "These are wonderful! Your arithmetic is of a very high standard, too, for a lad of your age. You should think about attending technical college when you're old enough. There is a bright future ahead of you."

Jack flushed at such unexpected praise, but he laughed a little too. Technical college? He was more likely to fly to the moon than attend college because he was going to be a carpenter. The Tregenna men had always been Penmarloe's carpenters, and their small workshop tucked away behind the fish market was as much a part of the small village as its cobbled lanes, steep-sided quay and keening gulls. Nobody in Penmarloe could remember a time before Tregennas had crafted waterwheels and newel posts. Every house in the parish, from Penmarloe Manor to the meanest fisherman's cottage, bore evidence of their skill. Jack had never questioned that his path might be any different – but now, as he glowed in the warmth of his teacher's praise, a door opened to a whole new world he'd never dreamed of, let alone imagined he might explore.

Jack had grown up watching his father work. Saul Tregenna was a master craftsman, and his work was much sought after; he was frequently commissioned by local gentry to fashion elegant staircases for great houses or to carve elaborate panelling for stylish drawing rooms. His latest commission was to create a rood screen for St Julietta's. This task was more than just a great honour – it also meant that the Tregenna family would have food on the table for several years ahead. Saul was delighted and set to work at once on a design, and Jack, as his apprentice, watched carefully as his father carved saints and fruits and delicate lattice work. It would be a piece as beautiful as any found in the greatest cathedral, for Saul Tregenna also had the soul of an artist and was, he often told Jack proudly, the Tregenna family's legacy.

Over the next few years the dedicated schoolmaster had continued to tutor Jack after class in the history of art, showing him more examples of famous sculptures and discussing Renaissance work and Neo-classicism with him while the other lads played football. Jack came to realise that his father was as much an artist as any Michelangelo, and although it was assumed that Jack would follow in the family tradition he dreamed of becoming a sculptor. Unable to practise on marble (a material in short supply in a Cornish fishing village) Jack honed his craft through wood carving and quietly planned his future as a sculptor. He would work his way around Europe, studying art in galleries and even finding work as an apprentice. He dreamed of learning to sculpt in Italy and of wandering the echoing corridors of the Louvre, and he could hardly wait to reach the advanced age of fourteen and leave school.

But Jack's dreams of the future perished with his father, and instead he left school to take over Saul's work. Fortunately Jack's skill as a carpenter was well known, so he was allowed to continue his father's commissions and the family were fed. By late summer in 1913 only the final section of the rood screen was left to be completed. This was the finest work Jack had ever done, and he was hugely proud of it. His studies of the great masters, and his hours poring over life drawing, had led to his creating a crucified Christ that would do justice to a Renaissance artist. The saints and coats of arms surrounding it were intricate and ornate. All that remained before it was completed were the final flourishes on the top section, but Jack was waiting for inspiration to strike. Only then would he pick up his tools and complete the piece, for this commission weighed heavily on him. In hundreds of years' time worshippers in St Julietta's would gaze up at his work. Maybe some would wonder about the man who created it. Others would feel moved as they worshipped. Some might even be inspired by it to seek God and His love. Such knowledge humbled Jack, and the responsibility quickened his heartbeat when he considered it too deeply. Although his own name would be lost with the turning of the tides and the relentless marching of the centuries, his work would live on for generations. This was why he would only complete the piece when he had the perfect final touch clear in his mind. He might not become a great sculptor, but St Julietta's rood screen would be his legacy. It was a work of art forever hidden in a small Cornish church.

As he clambered down the rocky path to the hidden cove where the village children always swam, Jack's thoughts were full of the incomplete screen. What could complete it? Mermaids? Waves bearing the ship which had carried Jesus and Joseph of Arimathea to England? Plump cherubs with their hands folded in prayer? None of these ideas excited him and, feeling frustrated, Jack decided to focus on his swim and hope inspiration would strike soon.

Jack glanced around to check he was alone, then he tugged off his shoes and socks before stripping down to his trousers. He was poised to discard these and launch himself into the water when a small dog hurtled down the path, barking wildly and wagging its plumy tail.

"Hello, there. Where have you come from?" Jack said. He didn't recognise this animal and as the dog leapt up at him Jack caught its collar. A small spaniel and, judging by its silky coat and the red velvet ribbon tied around its neck, a beloved pet rather than a working dog. He deduced this must be a lady's lapdog – which raised the question, where was the lady? Jack glanced around, but not a soul was in sight and the cove remained deserted. Was the owner injured on the cliff path with her ankle twisted, or had the wilful animal escaped, seeking adventures beyond the confines of velvet cushions and treats?

"I don't think you're meant to be here, are you?" Jack said to the spaniel, ruffling its ears. "Where's your mistress?"

In answer, the dog wriggled from his grasp and tore away

down the beach, dancing in and out of the waves. Worried it might be swept away, Jack sprinted along the tideline and scooped the spaniel up before it got itself into any more trouble. He would have to forgo his swim and search for the owner.

"Bramble! Oh, naughty boy! Bramble!"

The cry came from the top of the cliff path. Tucking the dog under one arm, Jack shielded his eyes with his free hand to see who was calling and his breath caught in his chest, for the most beautiful girl he had ever seen was silhouetted against the sky. Her hair spun gold in the sunlight and with her white dress floating behind her, she flew down the path like an angel descending from Heaven. Was she real or was this a dream?

"Bramble!" she cried. "Bramble!"

"I've got him, Miss!" Jack called, and he was amazed to hear that his voice sounded as calm as though he was speaking to the grocer rather than a goddess. "The path's very steep. Please don't rush!"

But the girl ignored him. Skirts bunched into her fists and buttoned boots skidding over the green-edged rocks, she hurried down to last few feet and jumped onto the wet sand. The spaniel wriggled free from Jack and leapt into her arms.

"Naughty dog," she sobbed, showering the wriggling spaniel with kisses. "Bramble, you bad boy to run away! Bad boy. Do you know how worried I was?"

Her cheeks were flushed, her nose was red and the hem of her dress was dirty and ripped by the gorse, but to Jack she still looked like an angel. His heart was thumping as though he was the one who'd given chase and his mouth as dry as though he'd swallowed half the beach. As language fled all he could think was how very much he longed to sketch her. The curve of her cheek and dark sweep of eyelashes against alabaster skin were pure perfection, and her full lips drew the eye as flowers enticed bees.

She was the missing piece from his rood screen. She was the one, and Jack knew there and then that he would never want to carve another face. She was his muse for all time.

"Thank you so much for catching him. I hope he didn't get you dirty?" the girl asked, glancing up at Jack through those thick black lashes. Even starred with tears and red with weeping, her unusual eyes, deep indigo ringed with the navy hue of a stormy sea, were strikingly beautiful, and Jack knew he was staring like a clot. She probably thought him a very rough and dull village lad, he thought despairingly, just as Estella had regarded Pip in *Great Expectations.* The schoolmaster had read this book to his pupils and Jack had never forgotten it, for just like Dickens' hero he too had high hopes and big dreams – and now, just like the unlucky Pip, he too had fallen head over heels in love with a girl as far above him in station as the moon and stars.

"He chased a seagull along the path and vanished over the edge. I thought he must have fallen," she continued, not appearing concerned that Jack was mute. He imagined such a beauty must have been used to having this effect on people. "I thought he must surely be dead."

As she said this her voice caught and her mouth trembled. Her lips were as pink and full as the petals of the roses Jack's mother grew around the porch, and he knew they would feel just as soft beneath his own, and would taste as sweet as honey. Roses and angels and bees. An angel with hair like spun gold and robes flowing like a waterfall. A cheek curved like a peach, and long lashes fanning them as her gaze was cast earthwards ...

A vivid image flickered through Jack's mind, as fleeting and as bright as the sunlight which spangled the waves, and his fingers tingled for his pencil. Angels with this girl's face. Flowing robes. Flowers thrumming with bees. Leaping dogs. Nodding grasses and sea pinks. A sweet smile that could light the darkest of nights. A perfect countenance that would grace a church for centuries.

It was her. She was the missing piece. She completed *everything.*

Unaware of Jack's racing thoughts and even faster racing heart, the girl ran her hands over the dog. "He isn't hurt, is he?"

Ambushed by her beauty, Jack was afraid that even the simplest of words would betray his longing. His tongue was knotted as though he had never conversed with a girl before – which was far from the truth. Broad-shouldered and well-muscled from lifting wood, and blessed with a mane of thick black curls and green eyes, Jack Tregenna was always the focus of female attention, and he was rarely lonely. The blacksmith's daughter was sweet on him and, with her wickedly slanting black eyes and lush curves that would make a saint contemplate sin, Jack wasn't averse to walking out with her. It was time he settled down, his mother often said, for he was almost eighteen now. Jack had agreed, but now he wanted to laugh at his own foolishness. Nobody else could compare to this girl. She was beautiful and brave and she moved his soul in a way he would never be able to explain. Jack might only be seventeen but now he knew all thoughts of other women were banished forever.

There would only ever be her.

Painfully aware that he was half-undressed, clad only in his dirty work trousers, Jack cleared his throat and sought the right words to explain his dishevelled state. She was clearly a lady and he knew that he should apologise for his rough appearance, yet she was still fussing over her dog and seemed oblivious to his bare-chested and grimy appearance. Nor did she appear concerned that he only was a village lad, for she chatted away happily to him, thanking him over and over again for his help.

"Bramble was chasing a gull one moment and then he vanished," she explained breathlessly. "I didn't see what happened next. Did he fall? Did you catch him?"

Jack shook his head. He took a deep breath and prayed language would return.

"No, Miss. He bolted down the cliff path. It's well-hidden and unless you knew where to look you wouldn't know there was a cove here, so it only looked as though he fell. Your dog's fine, I promise."

"Thank goodness," she said, hugging the spaniel tightly, oblivious to wet paws and sand. The dog yelped and wriggled out of her grasp, rolling over at Jack's feet with a volley of delighted barks.

Laughing, Jack scratched its belly. "You are a bad chap. You really frightened your mistress."

"He certainly did," she agreed. "I don't know what I'd do if anything happened to Bramble. He means the world to me."

It was plain to see just how much she loved the dog, and Jack felt quite jealous of the ungrateful Bramble. If he was the recipient of such adoration, Jack would never want to leave this girl's side!

"He's right as rain," he assured her, ruffling Bramble's ears before reaching into his pocket to pull out a hanky. "Please don't be distressed, Miss. Bramble's none the worse for his adventure, but I'd keep him on a leash in future since he likes to chase gulls. He might not be as lucky next time."

She took the cotton square from him and dabbed her eyes. "He's not a bad dog, it's just that he's never seen seagulls before. We're from Wimbledon – that's near London – and the seaside's new to both of us. Thank you so much for catching him before he ran off again. You've saved the day and you're an absolute hero."

Jack flushed. "Hardly. I was about to swim when he arrived and thew himself at me. I just got in the way. Would you excuse me if I fetched my shirt and shoes and got dressed?"

The deep blue gaze dropped to his chest, and it was as though she had seen him for the first time. Her cheeks coloured and she looked away, but not before her gaze had lingered on his torso and the corded muscles of his arms.

"Please do," she said primly. "Mr ... who is it I'm indebted to?"

"I'm Jack Tregenna," Jack said, shrugging on his shirt and buttoning it swiftly to spare her blushes. Truth be told, he was also feeling a little hot under the collar.

"Nice to meet you, Jack Tregenna, the rescuer of runaway dogs! I'm Caroline Sweethouse. My father's the new Rector," she said, holding out her hand.

"And you, Miss Sweethouse," Jack replied, although *nice* seemed an inadequate word to describe how bowled over he was by this unexpected encounter.

They shook hands and hers, gloved by his, fitted Jack's perfectly. Caroline inhaled sharply and Jack saw surprise flare in her eyes as she glanced up at him. She felt it too, he realised with a surge of delight. Whatever magic it was that drew him so powerfully to her was working both ways and

Jack was filled with the strongest conviction that their unexpected meeting was Fate's work.

Jack Tregenna and Caroline Sweethouse had always been destined to meet.

"Miss Sweethouse sounds terribly ancient," Caroline screwed up her nose at the name. Her hand still in his, Jack noticed. "It's Caro, by the way. That's what everyone calls me. Only my old nanny and Papa call me Caroline."

"Caro," Jack echoed. He loved the sound of her name and already adored the shape of it on his tongue. He could say it forever. As though in a dream he raised her hand to his lips and kissed it. "Welcome to Penmarloe, Caro."

She laughed at the formality and dropped a half-curtsey.

"Why, thank you! It's already proving far more exciting than Wimbledon! I think I'm going to like it here very much."

"As long as you keep Bramble on a lead," Jack warned.

"Oh, I shall," she promised. "I can't expect you to be here every time he chooses to misbehave."

Jack thought he would willingly exchange being a carpenter for a job watching out for Bramble. He was realistic enough to understand this was the closest a village lad like him could hope to come to a girl such as this. As Caro slipped her fingers from his and called the dog to heel, he looked about and marvelled that the beach and the cliffs and even the green smudge of the farthest headland appeared just as they always did. How was this possible, Jack wondered, when his world looked so very different now?

They climbed the steep path up from the rocky beach, making small talk about the village while Bramble zig-zagged ahead and barked at the gulls. When they reached the top Jack pulled off his belt and looped it through the spaniel's collar in case Bramble was tempted to dive into thin air once more. During their walk back to the village Caroline told Jack a little about herself and how she intended to go to university one day and become a teacher. She was as brilliant as she was beautiful, Jack thought in awe. When he explained that he was a carpenter, adding shyly that he had hoped to go away to study sculpture and art until his father's death had changed everything, Caro nodded sympathetically.

"It's hard when you lose a parent," she said, laying a hand on his arm in quiet understanding. "I miss Mama every day. Life is never the same again, is it?"

A boulder lodged in Jack's throat. He gulped and looked away, dangerously close to tears. He had never spoken to a soul about the loss of Saul Tregenna. He had never shared how much he missed hearing his father whistle in the workshop or described how he often felt frozen with disbelief that he would never see Saul again. Nothing, Jack had concluded, could prepare you for the unreality of death or explain how something so universal felt unique and as though you were the first person to experience it. Caro understood all this without the need to explain; he could see it in the shadows which filled her eyes when she had spoken about her mother and he had heard her voice catch. Like Jack's hopes of studying sculpture and art, Caro's dreams had also been shattered, for now she was needed to take care of her Papa, and running the Rectory was her responsibility. University was out of the question now, she sighed. How could she leave her dear Papa all alone?

They reached the Rectory, a graceful Georgian building placed neatly amid smooth lawns edged with clipped box hedges. This was where their brief meeting would end, for it was not for Jack to follow her. Behind the barley-sugar twists of the imposing wrought-iron gates, he spotted one of his old schoolfriends raking the gravel drive to perfection while another was at work trimming the wisteria, sharp reminders that his own place was at the back gate. Jack stepped backwards respectfully, twisting his cap in his hand and wishing that they didn't have to part. He could have spoken to Caro for a thousand years and never run out of conversation.

"Safely home," he said, nodding at Bramble. "Don't forget to use a leash in the future."

"How shall I return the belt? Shall I bring it to you?"

Jack's heart lifted. They both knew she was looking for a reason to see him again, since Bramble was safely inside the garden now. Caro's cheeks were flushed once more, and as she looked up at him her wide blue eyes were bright with urgency.

"I live on Fore Street. Our is the cottage at the end, and it has roses over the porch." *Pink ones like your lips*, he added silently.

"I'll find you," she said and they both knew she was making a promise about more than returning a belt. "Thank you again, Jack."

Then she was gone, her skirts whisking up the garden path before she leapt the steps to the front door and waved farewell. Jack remained at the gate staring after her for some time as though in a dream. Perhaps he *was* dreaming? He certainly felt as though he was sleepwalking back to the Tregennas' small cottage, and over supper his mother told him off several times for not listening to a word she'd said. Maud Tregenna was right; Jack scarcely heard her. All he could think about was Caro Sweethouse's hand in his, and basking in the warm sunshine of her smile. Until today he had only been half-alive, and even though the dusk was smoking in from the hillside and the candles were lit, he could hardly wait to escape to the workshop and begin work on the final section of the rood screen, for he knew exactly what he would carve into the dark oak.

Caro Sweethouse delivered the belt to the cottage the very next day. Maud was flattered and horrified in equal measure to have the new Rector's daughter visit her home. Although Caro was complimentary about the saffron buns and tea, conversation was awkward and once their visitor had departed, Jack's mother rounded on him.

"What were you thinking, son? Inviting the likes of her here?"

"She was only returning my belt. She told you all about what happened," Jack protested, but

Maud Tregenna snorted like the grocer's pony.

"Don't you nothing me, my boy! I know you, so take that daft look off your face right now. Caroline Sweethouse's not for the likes of you. Do you hear me? The Rector will want a curate for her at the very least."

He might not be a curate, Jack reflected five months later as the Christmas Eve congregation rose to utter the Lord's Prayer, but this hadn't mattered a jot to Caro. Nor did she care that he was a humble carpenter. By unspoken consent they hadn't met at Tregenna family's cottage again but at the cove, and this time with Bramble tethered by a lead and Jack more respectably attired. They talked easily and the afternoon flew by – as did the many meetings which followed. Caro loved art and painting and lent Jack books from her father's library, which he devoured. In turn he helped her improve her sketching and taught her where the best spots were to capture views or spot rare birds. They talked about their dreams, his of visiting Florence and Paris to see great sculpture, and Caro's of having independence and studying, and he would listen intently to her words of conviction that a big change was coming. She believed a time was approaching when class and birth and sex would matter far less than the person you were – and swept away by Caro's conviction, Jack began to share her optimism. Perhaps there was a chance for them after all?

Caro often visited the workshop to watch him carve. Sometimes Jack would go to find her in the church arranging flowers, or they would arrange to meet by chance while he was fitting the next section of the screen. They became good friends, and if Jack sometimes caught Caro studying him from beneath her lashes, his heart tumbling ever deeper as he yearned to hold her close and kiss her, he never dreamt of compromising her reputation.

There was only one solution to this, but following it required a huge feat of bravery on his part and a leap of faith and trust on hers. He loved her and he was certain that she loved him. Now he had to prove it, and once Midnight Mass was over he would do this. He would prove beyond any doubt to Caro that the way he felt about her was true and eternal.

Tonight he would lay his heart on the line. Tonight he would ask Caroline Sweethouse to become his wife.

3

1913
Cornwall
Jack

THE AIR WAS brittle with cold when the doors of the church opened, spilling light and villagers out into Christmas morning. As the bells sang out to declare the birth of Christ and St Julietta's rang with cries of 'Merry Christmas', Jack waited in his pew with his head bowed and hands folded reverently. Soon only he remained seated while the curate packed away the altar furniture. The Reverend Sweethouse retreated to the vestry to disrobe and Caro collected up the hymn books. Once they were alone, the curate departing with a cheerful wave and a Christmas blessing, she smiled the secret smile that always made Jack's heart swoop and which he knew was his alone.

"Merry Christmas, Jack," she said.

"Merry Christmas, Caro," Jack replied softly. His hand slid

into his pocket, resting on the small carving nestled deep within. He had created this especially for Caro. How he hoped she would like it and the secret it contained. His mouth became parched with a sudden rush of nerves. Was he fooling himself? Should he step away now?

Caro placed her pile of hymn books on a shelf and pulled her coat closer, shivering in the chill. "My, it's bitter tonight. I wouldn't be surprised if we had snow for Christmas Day."

Without the press of bodies crammed into pews the church had grown colder but even with a blue nose and bundled up in a thick coat and scarf she was achingly beautiful. How Jack longed to kiss her.

"Best we get home and into the warm," he said.

Caro nodded. "I'm ready, but Papa will be a while yet finishing up. He likes to pray alone on Christmas Eve. I've learned not to wait up for him, and so has our housekeeper. He'll be at least another hour."

Her meaning was clear: they would be able to enjoy a few moments alone. Since the Rectory was next door to the church it was perfectly respectable for Caro to walk the short distance unescorted, and nobody would think twice if they saw her accompanied by Jack Tregenna, also on his way home. This was how they often managed to spend time together – precious snatched fragments comprised of their 'chance' meetings in the village or at the church – and it was these moments that Jack lived for. He collected the memory of each one, and treasured them as though they were a hoard of precious jewels he could pore over when he was alone, turning each one over and reliving it in minute detail. How he ached to tell Caro how he felt about her!

He just couldn't wait for a time when he and Caro could openly be together and walk arm in arm through the village.

He had worked hard these past months, taking on extra commissions and working late into the night in order to save up and prove to Reverend Sweethouse that he was worthy of his daughter. His reputation was growing, and only yesterday he had been commissioned by Lord and Lady Carlyon to create a fine new staircase for their great house. He would need to take on an apprentice at this rate, and find a bigger premises to house the workshop. He would easily be able to provide for a wife, Jack thought proudly. All he had to do now was find the courage to propose.

His stomach cartwheeled again. Was he brave enough to do this?

Jack followed Caro outside and into the churchyard, which had emptied now as the villagers scurried home to warm up by the fire. The inky sky was sprayed with bright stars and a slice of moon silvered the soft mounds of ancient tombs and cast shadows over the sleeping world. Frost crackled beneath boots as they strolled along the path, more frost sparkling on railings and icing grass like the diamond ring Jack longed to give Caro. He touched his pocket again and drew courage from the solid wood beneath his fingertips. It would bring him luck – how could it not?

Jack had carved an angel bearing Caro's own face. It was a prototype of the dozens he had created to adorn the rood screen and he knew it was special. Something told him that this angel would watch over him now and in the days that followed.

Once they were far enough from the church for its lights to be just a glow and no prying eyes could see them, Jack took Caro's gloved hand in his and drew her against his heart. With the moonlight caressing her tilted face and the iced world sparkling all around them he felt as though he was in a strange and wonderful new land where anything and everything was possible.

"There's something I need to say to you," he began, surprised that his voice sounded so even since inside he was trembling like leaves in an autumn storm. "From the first moment I saw you I knew you were like nobody I'd ever met before."

She laughed. "Because I came tearing down a cliff path and interrupted your quiet swim and caught you half-dressed?"

"I blame Bramble for that," Jack said, rolling his eyes at the memory. "But I've forgiven him. In fact, I owe Bramble a great deal for running away that day, otherwise we might never have become friends."

Caro leaned into him and rested her head against his chest. "Yes indeed. I can't imagine *not* being your friend, Jack."

"Even though our backgrounds are so different? When I'm a carpenter and you're the Rector's daughter?"

It was the old fear – the small crack in the earth between them that he feared might become a canyon which would swallow him whole. With his dreams of studying art long since dashed, Jack knew there was little he could offer Caroline Sweethouse apart from his heart. That had belonged to Caro since the moment he'd first laid eyes on her – but was it enough?

Caro frowned. She hated it when he raised the subject of rank and status. "You know my thoughts on all that. It's who we are inside that truly counts, Jack, not some accident of birth. You're clever and kind and talented, and if the world was a fair place you'd have left here long ago and already made a name for yourself. A time's coming when birth and class won't matter a jot, and when men, and women too, will make their own way on their own merits. You'll see."

She had told him this many times, but Jack couldn't imagine what might turn the world upside down so greatly that this might be the case. There was surely nothing powerful enough?

"The more time I spend with you the more I know you're a wonderful person," Caro continued. "You've a true talent, Jack. You're clever and creative, but most of all you're loyal to your family and put them first, even if doing so has cost you your dreams. That matters far more to me than whether you're a carpenter or a duke. I can't begin to tell you how much I admire you."

He shrugged, embarrassed. "Anyone would do the same."

"They wouldn't," Caro insisted. "A lot of people would have left their family to fend for themselves and followed their own inclinations. That's what I love about you the most, I think, your generous, kind heart. Oh Jack, don't you see? Our actions and our hearts show our true worth, not what we own or our worldly rank." She pressed the heel of her hand against her chest. "It's what we feel and who we are in *here* that counts. Nothing else."

Jack stared at Caro. Had he heard her correctly? She loved him?

"That's what you *love* about me?" he whispered, hardly daring to hope.

She nodded shyly, but her eyes were sparkling like the Christmas stars. "Of course I love you, Jack Tregenna. Surely you know that? Isn't it obvious?" She tipped her head back and laughed up at his surprised expression. "Oh, Jack! You ninny! I felt sure you must know!"

"I never even dared to hope," he said, shaking his head. "I

love you too, Caro. I've loved you since the moment I first saw you."

"And I you," she said softly, reaching up to cup his cheek. "And every moment since."

Then, and just as he'd longed to do for so long, Jack dipped his head and touched his lips to hers in a snowflake-soft kiss. Caro leaned into him, resting one small hand on the lapel of his overcoat, and kissed him back tentatively. It was a soft and gentle first kiss and one that spoke of promises and endless joys ahead. Jack had never dreamed anything could be as wonderful as this tender kiss, for it was filled with quiet peace like the relief of reaching a calm harbour after a long and uncertain voyage.

When they drew apart, Jack understood that this was the moment he had been born for. His heart was thudding as though he was about to dive off a high rock but even so he'd never felt more certain of anything in his life. He slid his hand into his pocket and as he did so his trembling fingers closed around the carved angel.

"I have something for you," he said shyly. "I made it especially for this evening."

Caro's hand flew to her throat as Jack drew a carved angel from his pocket and offered it to her. It wasn't large, no more than seven inches tall, but it was carved as intricately and with as much care as any that graced the rood screen he was still slaving over. Maybe this angel had been carved with even more care, because she was for his beloved Caroline. Jack had spent hours perfecting this piece, abandoning several earlier versions because of a flaw in the wood that irked him or because the form hadn't taken life quite as he wished – but this final angel was perfect, from the flowing folds of her wooden gown to the tips of her feathered wings. She was the best work Jack had ever done, and the closest thing to a sculpture he might ever achieve.

Yes, Jack thought with a glow of satisfaction when he finally laid his tools down, this angel was perfect, because she looked exactly like the girl he loved.

"It's me!" Caro whispered, looking up at him with tear filled eyes. "Oh Jack! She has my face!"

Jack nodded. "Yes."

She spun the angel around in her hands, shaking her head in amazement.

"This is your finest work. It's exquisite. Oh! You're wasted as a carpenter!"

Jack laughed. "I'm not sure that's true. But you talked about how you see me, Caro, and this is how I see you. You're my angel from heaven."

She blushed at this. "I'm no angel, Jack. I'm as human and as flawed as anyone."

But Jack refused to accept this. He took her in his arms and kissed her again and for a while they thought of little else but speaking this whole new language of touch and wonder.

"Remember the day we met?" he murmured eventually into her hair. "I wasn't sure how I would ever manage without my father, or even if I could. My dreams were in ashes, and I thought that everything I had ever hoped for was over. Then you appeared on the cliffs and my world changed in a heartbeat. I've never carved and created like I have since I met you, Caro. You're my muse. You've unlocked me. I can't wait to show you the finished rood screen."

"I can't wait to see it. It's a work of art, Jack. It should be in the Louvre, not our church!"

"I can make another for the Louvre," he said. "I can do anything with you beside me. You're the girl I love. You're *my* angel." He leaned in again to kiss her parted lips – a kiss that was as light as the carved angel's feathery wings – then he leaned his forehead gently against Caro's. This was it. He couldn't delay a second longer, because such a magical night, pincushioned with stars and lanced with spear-sharp air, might never come again.

This was the moment he had been waiting for. "Look inside," he said.

"Inside?"

"Inside the angel. There's a secret hiding place which opens if you slide the bottom here, see?"

Jack took Caro's hands in his, guiding them over the base of the angel until a hidden catch was sprung and a secret compartment revealed. It had taken him an age to design and perfect the mechanism and he was delighted with it. Nobody would know it was there unless they looked very closely.

"Oh!" she exclaimed, holding it up to see. "How clever!"

"You can store trinkets or jewellery inside," he suggested, but Caro had a better idea.

"It's perfect for hiding leaflets about women's suffrage."

She was always reading pamphlets and penning her own ideas – work which she knew her father would veto if he ever found it – and Jack was pleased she had found a use for his angel that was close to her heart.

Then Caro's brows drew together as she shook the angel and heard a rattle. "Wait! There's something inside."

There was another rattle followed by a gasp as a ring fell into Caro's open palm. A small diamond sparkled like the first Christmas star, and Caro stared at it in disbelief. This ring had cost Jack more money than he dared admit, plus the pain of pawning the fob watch left to him by his father, but when he saw the joy in Caro's eyes he knew it was worth every penny.

"Is this what I think it is?" she asked.

In answer, Jack dropped to his knees. "Caro, I—"

"Get up!" Caro attempted to haul him from the frozen earth. "You'll catch a chill, you idiot!"

But Jack stayed put, little caring about such things as chills. It didn't matter a jot to him that the earth was hard and cold or that he might look a fool. He was far too busy dredging up the courage to speak.

"Will you marry me?" he blurted, gripping her gloved hands tightly. "I know I don't have a great deal to offer you, and that I'm only a carpenter and you could aim far higher, but I swear that all I have and am and ever will be is yours. If you'll have me, I'll spend the rest of my life loving you, cherishing you and caring for you. Not a day will pass when you are not foremost in my thoughts."

In answer Caro fell to her knees too and flung her arms around his neck.

"Of course I will!" she laughed, hugging him. "Oh Jack! I was so scared you'd let all the other things get in the way. I never dreamed this would happen tonight!"

Jack couldn't quite believe his ears. "You'll marry me? You're saying yes?"

"Yes! Yes! Yes!" Caro cried, and they fell into one another's arms, laughing and kissing and oblivious to the cold earth. "Of course, I'll marry you Jack Tregenna! Try and stop me!"

The stars seemed to shine all the more brightly then, and the whole world sparkled for Jack and Caro. This was the most enchanted Christmas Eve ever, and Jack knew he would remember it for ever. As he kissed Caro again, he promised to carve her an angel every Christmas for the rest of their lives.

She would have dozens of them, because they would grow old and grey together and it would be their special way of remembering this most wonderful of Christmas Eves.

"I'll need to speak to your father," Jack said as, arm in arm, they rejoined the path which wound between the graves. The church was still lit up, jewelled windows bright in the darkness, and the Rector would be within. Maybe Jack should speak to him straight away? It was only right that he should do so, and as soon as possible.

"You will," agreed Caro, pulling a face. "It's utter nonsense, of course, because this is *my* decision, but there you are. Men still believe that women have little say in such matters. One day that'll change, but not in time to save you from having to speak to Papa, I'm afraid."

"Should I do it now?" A little like pulling a tooth, Jack thought it might be best to get this over with.

"Papa might be a little tired tonight and that makes him grumpy. Maybe tomorrow? Once he has eaten his Christmas dinner and enjoyed some port. He'll be in an amenable mood by then," she said.

"I hope so, because he'll know his daughter could do far better than the village carpenter," Jack sighed.

If only he had more to offer Caro. Jack swore he would work hard, and he would always give her everything he could, but he was also realistic enough to know that the Reverend Sweethouse would not be delighted by the union. The Rector would rightly believe that his daughter could aim far higher.

"Papa knows you're honest and hardworking," Caro reassured him. "And anyway, Jesus was a carpenter. He can hardly argue with that!"

Jack laughed at this, and kissed her again. Then they

walked over to the Rectory, stealing kisses whenever the moon slipped behind a wisp of cloud, and making excited plans. They would marry the very next Christmas Eve, for Caro thought this would give Jack enough time to save up and for her to organise her trousseau. It also meant that their wedding anniversary would always be a reminder of this beautiful night. They could scarcely wait.

By the time they reached the Rectory gates the lights in all the cottage windows were extinguished and only the stars lit their way. Jack and Caro were alone in a Christmas kingdom, where ice tinkled in the air, frosted grass crackled beneath their boots and owls' calls shivered from the woods. The future ahead was as bright and as sparkling as the wintry world, and they both agreed that next Christmas couldn't come soon enough. 1914 was going to be a year that would change their lives for ever ...

4

The Present
London
Ellen

It was late afternoon by the time Ellen arrived home from Clara's house, but already the day had retreated as twilight billowed in from darkening streets and the deep purple expanse of the park. As it was a little too early for curtains to be drawn and blinds lowered, the windows of the houses flanking the pavements were stage sets boasting Christmas scenes illuminated for the benefit of passers-by. Truncated basement windows hurled slices of light at booted feet, drawing eyes downwards to catch tantalising glimpses of lamplit subterranean worlds.

The contrast of these cosy scenes with her own bare flat was almost shocking. As she shut the door and shrugged off her coat, the lack of decorations and festive cheer in her own home seemed stark. A few Christmas cards were displayed half-heartedly on the top shelf of a bookcase and the coffee table was laden with the presents she was still to wrap, but otherwise the place looked much as it always did – or rather as it had since Steve had moved out and Clara had become unwell. The flat was somewhere to sleep and to heat up a microwave meal for one. It was somewhere to sleep the dreamless sleep that followed weeks of nursing a loved one. Ellen realised her flat was less a home and more of a place to hide away.

The place felt empty and unloved. Ellen had spent so little time there in recent months that it had taken on a neglected air. Dust that she hadn't had the time or inclination to flick away gathered on the surfaces, a pile of post teetered on the kitchen counter, and the fridge was almost empty. Black coffee it was, then, Ellen decided as she closed the fridge door, and a takeaway tonight. Or maybe just toast? Like putting up a tree and decorations, there seemed little point in shopping and cooking for one.

When she and Steve had been together he'd happily taken charge of the Christmas decorations and Ellen had teased him that his efforts would distract the planes landing at Heathrow. No possible spot for fairy lights, tinsel and baubles had been neglected, and even the elderly cherry tree in the garden had been festooned. He'd been only a trip to B&Q away from rigging up a giant Santa complete with flashing sleigh and reindeer, Ellen recalled with a fond smile, and his tree had been a work of art. A primary school teacher, Steve threw himself into all the celebrations with gusto, and she imagined that his classroom would be spectacular as always and his new girlfriend's place transformed into Santa's grotto. More of a minimalist herself, Ellen thought this was a reminder that she and Steve had never been destined to go the distance.

Coffee made and the fire lit, Ellen pulled the curtain to shut out the night and curled up on the sofa with her drink. The flames dancing in the woodburner were cheery and lent the room an air of welcome. Her garden flat, part of a conversion of an Edwardian town house, boasted a wealth of original features that sent visitors into paroxysms of joy. With the large fireplace, high ceilings and sash windows, it came into its own at Christmas time. Maybe she ought to buy a tree, Ellen thought. Just a small one with some elegant white lights to soften the place and hint at Christmas. Granny Clara would have approved of this idea, and it seemed right to Ellen that she should do something in memory of her and to celebrate the time of year she'd loved so much.

Maybe Anna was right and she ought to have some fun? It wasn't too late to change her mind. Ellen picked up her phone to scroll through the list of recent calls. Her thumb hovered over Anna's name, but it was hard to dredge up any the enthusiasm for crowds, loud music and celebrations. Tomorrow she would help Maggie finish clearing Clara's house, and then everything was done and life would settle down into a new normal. Until then, a quiet evening in, a bubble bath and maybe a glass of wine – one of the few things Ellen did have in her fridge – were just what she needed.

She laid the phone down on the coffee table and closed her eyes. She needed time to grieve for Clara and to heal slowly and gradually. Anna meant well, and a time would come when Ellen would join her, might even look to start dating again, but that time would present itself. It would not be forced. It would happen naturally and when she was ready.

She must have fallen asleep in the warmth and the soft lamp light, for it seemed only moments later that her phone buzzed with an incoming text message. Ellen blinked and reached for it, expecting a plea from Anna attempting to persuade her to come out, but it was a message from her mother.

Just remembered – Granny Heidi said Grandpa owed his life to the angel, whatever that means. I seem to remember he went spare when the family dog ran off with it one Christmas! Sabine might know more. Will call her asap x

The lost angel! In her exhausted state Ellen had forgotten her find, but as she read her mother's message fascination ignited in her imagination, chasing sleep away and filling her with a fizz of curiosity. The angel was a link to Granny Clara, but more than that – she was also a link to her own past and the roots of Ellen's family, roots that were deeply entwined in the rich soil of another land and culture. If it hadn't been for the recent scurry to get post-Brexit EU passports, and the bittersweet memories of Clara's Christmas traditions, Ellen wondered whether she would have thought much at all about her family's German heritage. She was saddened that Clara would never be able to tell her more about her childhood in Germany. So many stories and memories were lost forever. Maybe the lost angel was one story that Ellen could salvage? A link to her great-grandparents that would be saved from time's shifting sands.

Ellen hauled herself from the sofa to retrieve the angel from her bag. The soft light smoothed the chips in the wooden face and softened the garish paint. Ellen made a fresh coffee and sat down once more, with the angel resting on the arm of the sofa. It hadn't been her imagination; this really was an exquisite piece. It might have been cobbled together from odds and ends, but these were materials which must have been swooped upon with delight by somebody with an eye for detail. An artist had made this angel, for the proportions were perfect and the carving skilled. Had her great-grandfather, Heinrich, whittled it to pass the tense hours between waking and combat? Or a comrade of his perhaps, desperate to distract himself from the mud and shells and all the other horrors of the First World War, horrors that had become part of popular culture thanks to the poems of Owen and Sassoon? Or had Heinrich bought it as a keepsake from a French craftsman? Ellen would never know its origins, but she hoped the little angel could be a means of knowing a little more about her family's past and keeping Granny Clara close.

She could clean the angel up and make it beautiful again. The paint would come off if she found the right solvent, and although there were a couple of bite marks at the top of the carved head, courtesy of the long-ago naughty pet, she could smarten it up and make it fit to grace the top of a Christmas tree once again. This would be her incentive to go out and buy one and decorate the flat, Ellen decided. She would do this for the lost angel. It wouldn't be a giant tree, but something elegant and in a pretty pot. A miniature tree sprinkled with white lights to twinkle and sparkle and soften the room, and which would suit the little angel. Ellen felt a tingle of excitement. *See*? She could hear Clara say. *You can still enjoy Christmas*.

Maybe she could find a way to change the rough hessian robe, too? Some floaty netting or some lace would be perfect. Ribbons for a sash, crimson and green for a festive look. She could check out one of the fabric stalls at the market and meet Anna for hot chocolate and Christmas shopping. Her grandmother would have been so pleased, and although she knew it was just her imagination it seemed to Ellen that the angel's sweet smile brightened too.

"Perhaps we're helping each other?" Ellen said to the angel.

Heartened by this plan, she tipped the angel upside down to examine her more closely. It oughtn't to be very hard to make some alterations and as her mother had pointed out, since the angel wasn't valuable she would only be improving it. Although the robe was loose and frayed in places, beneath this first layer was a second one made from the same rough fabric, wrapped snugly around the wooden waist and tightly secured with tiny stitches. This underlayer was grubby and stained and, as far as Ellen could see, had never been removed. How strange to think that the person who'd once stitched this into place with such care was long gone yet their work remained. What stories would this angel tell if she could speak?

After calling Anna and arranging to meet in town the following morning, Ellen was keen to begin work on the angel. She made some toast, discovering that she was unusually hungry, and after wolfing it down fetched her nail scissors and sat at the kitchen table with the main light on so she could snip all the stitches without causing any damage. With the cosy chatter of the television in the background and the thrill of a project to engross her, Ellen felt happier than she had for a long time. It was a little fanciful, but it really felt to her as though Granny Clara had sent this angel and made sure that as Ellen was clearing away it had found its way to her.

The sharp tips of the scissors soon snipped away the threads which had kept the coarse fabric in place for decades. The robe disintegrated in Ellen's hands but to her surprise the layers beneath it were well preserved and were wrapped several times around the angel's trunk. Even the base had been bound tightly. She unwound curls of fabric until the angel was free from her swaddling. Ellen ran her hands over it, frowning when she discovered the wood had been hacked into. Closer examination revealed a deep gash in the trunk as though the tip of a sharp blade had pierced it. Her mother as a child, let loose with scissors? Surely not. This slash had to have been created by a very sharp blade, and with some force too.

Puzzled, Ellen continued studying her find. There was something at the base, an indentation that was not damage like the deeply scored groove, but smooth and pleasing to the touch. It appeared as though it was crafted into the piece and Ellen's fingers probed the wood. Goodness! Something felt like a catch. She pressed down with her thumb and heard a soft click, followed by the base of the trunk springing open.

There was a hidden compartment in the angel!

Ellen gasped, for this secret drawer couldn't have been opened since the creator of this ornament had sealed up its secrets with the rough hessian and tight stitches. It was the perfect hiding place, for nobody would have ever thought to look for one there. Only the person who'd fashioned the angel would know there was a concealed place within – unless the secret was shared. It had never been shared with her great-grandfather, of this Ellen felt certain, and as her fingers explored the compartment she wondered if this meant that the angel had never been intended to be his?

There was something tucked inside. It felt like paper

folded over and over to make it small enough to be secreted away. Ellen eased it out with her fingernail and saw that she was right – there was paper hidden inside, age-yellowed and crackly. As she unfolded it she saw that it was a letter, the page covered in neat handwriting as though the author was desperate to make use of every millimetre of paper:

The Rectory, Church Lane, Penmarloe, November 4th, 1914

My darling Jack,

Today I read the newspaper reports of how it is for you in France and I am so very afraid, especially since I suspect they dare not tell us how bad it really is for you all. My darling, I am so frightened that I will never see you again and I long for you every minute of every day. I think about you all the time and I ache for your kisses and your touch.

Ellen looked up from the yellowed page. These intimate words had clearly never been intended for the eyes of Heinrich Schmidt and even though the intended recipient would have passed away many, many years ago Ellen knew she was intruding on something very private. This was a love letter written by a woman to the man she loved, a man who must have known the remainder of his life was counted in days rather than years. Ought she to read on? Was this any of her business?

On the other hand, she argued, it was all such a long time ago and this was history. Whoever this Jack was who had received the letter had hidden it inside the angel for safekeeping, and the angel had somehow gone to her own great-grandfather, Heinrich. The unknown Jack's story must have been linked to that of Heinrich, the schoolteacher who fought in the trenches and who, by all accounts, had never recovered from the horror. This was his story too, then, and Clara's, and ultimately her own.

But they would have been enemies – so how could Heinrich have come by this angel? Ellen knew she had to read the letter if she wanted to know more. "Read on!" she heard Clara saying, standing at her shoulder and urging her to continue. "See what it says, Elly! What have you got to lose?"

Ellen had never been able to refuse her grandmother anything. She smoothed the paper flat on the table top and leaned forward, squinting at the cramped and faded writing. Then she took a deep breath and began to read ...

5

December 1914
Cornwall
Caro

WHEN THE ACHE of Jack's absence was too much to bear, Caro sought solace in the church. She was not alone in this; women were often to be found in St Julietta's these days, hands folded and faces pale as they prayed for their menfolk so far away at the Front. But Caro did not come to church to plead with God to bring Jack Tregenna safely home to her. Nor did she find comfort in prayers or the reassurance of victory in her father's sermons. Instead, she would visit St Julietta's because it was here she felt closest to her fiancé, and the church was a place where she wouldn't be interrupted by the housekeeper or the demands of parishioners. Neither could the telegram boy bicycle through the nave, the mere glimpse of his jaunty hat enough to turn her blood into an icy waterfall. So here she could enjoy a few moments of respite from the stalking dread that was her constant companion these days.

In the church Caro was left in peace to gather her thoughts; nobody would interrupt the Reverend's daughter here. She could gaze up at the newly installed rood screen, finished mere weeks before Jack Tregenna kissed her goodbye on the platform, shouldered his kitbag and boarded the train with all the other young men from the surrounding area. She felt soothed by the knowledge that the skilled hands which had fashioned the elaborate carvings above were the same hands that had caressed her face with such tenderness, and being close to Jack's work helped her feel closer to him. Like the gleaming wood, she was also a thousand times richer for his touch.

Jack Tregenna had poured his soul into this rood screen, and so it must surely contain some essence of the man she loved. His warm laughter was etched in the mischievous smile of every cherub, his deep love of nature carved into so many of the tendrils of vine and coils of ivy; and the lines of his strong and lean body were echoed in the limbs of his carved Christ figure. There was comfort in knowing his work would endure long after their faces were forgotten, and it was a reminder that no matter how unbearable the present was, a day would come when the war was no more than a chapter in a history book. Everything rose and everything fell. Each man, and woman, had their season.

As she slipped into her pew on the raw afternoon of Christmas Eve in 1914, an afternoon that was as bleak as she felt, Caro was certain that whatever came next, no matter how difficult the months ahead would be, she was blessed to love

Jack Tregenna and she was honoured to be his fiancée. He had brought her so much happiness in the short time they had known one another, and as she spun her engagement ring around on her left finger, a gesture which had become a nervous habit, her heart was warmed by the remembrance of happiness she'd felt when Jack had presented her with his carved angel. The ring was much looser these days, but it sparkled as brightly as ever.

Would Jack come safely home to her? Surely they would be granted that much? Fate, God, Destiny, call it whatever you will, could surely not be so cruel as to divide them so soon, thought Caro. But Penmarloe's streets were filled with women dressed in the sombre hues of mourning and she knew the odds were stacked against the two of them. This war cared little for lovers, and even less for the hopes and dreams of the young people it had divided.

The news from the Front grew bleaker every day and rather than the war being over by Christmas, as they had all been naïvely promised, it seemed doomed to limp into another miserable year and maybe beyond even that. The Reverend Sweethouse never attempted to pretend otherwise to Caro; he respected his daughter's intellect far too much to feed her platitudes. Being well read, she was painfully aware of the horrors Jack and the other soldiers faced on the front line. Maybe they should have married before he left for the training camp, Caro fretted, as she twisted her ring around and around. Lots of young couples had done so, but Jack had insisted they wait, to do things properly when he returned on leave.

"I promised your father I would take care of you," he had told Caro the day before he was due to leave for the training camp in Sussex. They sat on the cliffs watching the waves dash against the rocks below, and although she held his hand tightly, Caro sensed that he was already slipping away from her, his thoughts in France and on the duty which lay ahead.

"With my army wages put aside, I can do that properly. Why, we can have our own cottage rather than having to share with Ma and the girls."

Caro, who would rather have shared a house with the entire village than see Jack enlist, sighed. This was a discussion they'd had dozens of times and she already knew his mind was made up. "I don't mind that. I've said so often enough. You don't need to enlist. There's enough men who want to fight."

"*I* mind," he said softly.

"But you're not a soldier! You're a carpenter!" Caro didn't mean to shout but she was frustrated, and fear sharpened her tongue "Don't you love me enough to stay?"

"I love you more than anything, Caro, but I have to do my bit. How can I stand back while other men do their duty for King and country? I couldn't live with myself. If the Kaiser seizes the French and Belgian coast, we're done for. All this" – he swept his arm in the direction of the village, cottages tumbled over the headland, bathed in honeyed sunshine and bursting with late summer's ripeness – "all this is done for. Gone."

"But you'd be safe," Caro whispered.

"But at what cost? I'd be a safe coward who stood back while others did their duty." Jack shook his head wearily. "Could you truly love and respect such a man?"

Caro thought she could have loved Jack through anything. Besides, this war was not their war. They had no argument with the Prussians, and although Caro was an intelligent young woman even she struggled to make sense of how the events in faraway Sarajevo had escalated into this dreadful conflict almost on their doorstep. Yet she also knew that the man she loved was honourable and brave and loved his country. How could she ask Jack to deny his very nature and hide away from what his conscience told him was the right course of action? She knew if she did it would poison everything.

"I just want us to be married," Caro said, and her throat tightened because she had already known what his decision would be. "I want us to be together, Jack."

He drew her against him and she rested her head on his shoulder, leaning into him and loving the strength of his arm as it held her close. She wished she could stay there for ever.

"And we will be, my love. This war will be over by Christmas; everyone agrees on that. We've set our wedding date for Christmas Eve and I'll be home by then. I promise."

Caro bit back a sharp retort that said Jack could no more promise this than he could reach up and pluck out the stars or demand the tides to cease turning. She knew he only wanted to reassure her.

"And your father approves of my enlistment," he continued, mistaking her bitter silence for agreement. "He's almost forgiven me for being a tradesman now I'm doing my bit. That I've been made a lieutenant has really helped my cause."

Caro rolled her eyes. Her Papa was such a snob sometimes. So much for God making all men equal!

"Best not tell him it was only because Colonel Rivers put in a good word for me," Jack added with a grin. "He must have really been impressed with the newel post I made for Rosecraddick Manor."

"His son was impressed with *you*," Caro pointed out loyally.

Kit, the Colonel's son and heir, had been very taken with Jack's ability. Although they were far apart in rank the two young men had enjoyed several conversations about art while Jack oversaw the staircase renovations. It was Kit's doing that the Colonel's old regiment had accepted Jack as a lieutenant – although Caro wasn't certain whether she wanted to thank him or throttle him for this. It was true that her father was delighted and that Jack would earn a good wage, but he would also be in dreadful danger. She would lie awake at night with her heart racing and a swelling sense of panic which refused to be dissolved by the sunlight.

"Either way, it helped our cause. You can't deny it," Jack said, and Caro scowled, for he was right. If such an illustrious family as the Rivers had approved of Jack Tregenna, the Reverend Sweethouse was not inclined to argue.

As Jack had feared, the Reverend Sweethouse had been far from delighted to discover that his daughter was being courted by the village carpenter. When Jack had plucked up the nerve to ask him for her hand in marriage, the Rector's roar of fury was so loud that Caro, listening at the study door, had jumped backwards in alarm and Betty the maid had dropped the teapot she was carrying to the drawing room. As Caro swept up china and mopped Earl Grey from the tiled floor, poor Jack backed out of the Rector's study, ashen-faced and with his cap clutched tightly in shaking hands. It had been a bruising encounter.

"I think that might have gone a little better," he said shakily. "Your father wants you to marry a man with prospects, Caro, and he isn't willing to give me his permission."

"*You* have prospects. You have your own business and you are going to become a sculptor," Caro reminded him staunchly. Permission indeed! How dare Papa? She wasn't a piece of luggage to be claimed! Scowling, she swept the final shards of china into a dustpan which she passed to Betty, before taking Jack's shaking hands in hers.

"Leave Papa to me," she said, squeezing his fingers tightly. "His bark is worse than his bite. He'll come around, you'll see."

Jack, who looked as though he had been savaged, was doubtful, but he still had no idea just how persuasive Caroline Sweethouse could be when she put her mind to it. His intended also had a mind that was sharper than the knifing draughts which blew through the ancient church in December, and her doting father found it hard to deny his only child anything.

Hadn't he, her own dear Papa, always taught her that God saw into men's hearts? Was it not true that only He could judge a man? Judge not less ye shall be judged? The Lord knew that Jack Tregenna was honest and true, Caro argued. God saw into men's hearts and God alone judged. Jack was well thought of in the village: he was a master craftsman, owned a flourishing business to boot, and if circumstances had been different would have been abroad studying and making a name for himself as a sculptor. But most of all she loved him and she wanted to marry him. Caro wouldn't settle for anyone else. Not ever.

If she couldn't marry Jack Tregenna then she would die an old maid.

Her father steepled his fingers beneath this chin and

regarded his determined daughter over the top of his pince-nez. "Very impressive sentiments, my dear, but I thought your heart was set on studying? What about your ambitions to read the Greats, hmm? How will you do that if you're a carpenter's wife? How will you look after any children?"

Caro had already thought long and hard about this for it was, in fairness to her father, a big consideration. She had never intended to fall in love, and until that summer afternoon when Bramble had chosen to run away she had been perfectly content with her books and studies. All this had changed when Jack's sea-green eyes met hers. Her world had turned upside down and her plans were turned inside out.

Caro still longed to study. She wanted this desperately – but she also wanted to be Jack's wife. Why must the two be exclusive, she thought mutinously. Why couldn't a woman study *and* be a wife? Well, they could! Perhaps she would be the first.

Caro had read enough pamphlets on women's suffrage and female emancipation to believe with all her heart that a time was coming when such feats would be possible – normal even. Jack agreed, and he was keen for her to follow her dream. Although she wouldn't be able to matriculate – another unfairness due to her sex which made her want to scream – she could still study. She had a sizeable inheritance from her grandfather that would become hers when she was twenty-one, and she and Jack had agreed that this would fund her time at St Anne's. The logistics they would worry about at a later date.

"I'll still study, Papa," Caro said firmly. "Jack supports me in that. He knows that I want to teach."

Reverend Sweethouse raised his eyebrows. "He may feel

differently once you are his *wife*, my dear, and so might you. You will have new responsibilities."

"We'll manage," she insisted, hands on her hips. "We can do this, Papa. You have to trust me."

Her father sighed. Young people would always follow their hearts and ignore the advice of their elders. It had been that way since Adam and Eve, and his cherished and, he had to admit, indulged daughter was no different. Caro was a determined young woman and when she set her mind on something she would rarely change course. Her mama had been just the same, of course, and lucky for him that she had been. He recalled that her father, a baronet, had been most unamused when his daughter announced she wished to marry the curate.

Beaten, Reverend Sweethouse gave in – albeit with much grumbling that Caro ought to have been a boy and studied law since she was so gifted at arguing – and granted his blessing. The wedding day was set for Christmas Eve, Jack promising to carve another angel which would guard their wedding rings, and soon Caro hadn't been able to think of anything more than dresses and flowers and her trousseau. She had been so happy to be marrying Jack and so caught up in their plans that the events in Europe crept up on her and had totally taken her by surprise.

Now, in the bitter cold of that Christmas Eve, she studied the church's stained-glass window, illuminated by a thin ray of sun from a watery winter sunset, and marvelled that there had ever been a time when fear hadn't cast a shadow over her every waking moment and when the newspapers hadn't contained lists of the dead. Jack was a junior officer at the Western Front, far away from Cornwall. Although his letters were cheerful, filled with funny stories about the disgusting bully beef and the antics of his comrades, she detected the exhaustion and the fear threaded through each line. The letters were sporadic, and parts were often redacted, but Caro was no fool; she understood that the conditions the men lived and fought in were hell on earth. Sometimes Jack mentioned pals of his and included anecdotes about the japes they got up to when they weren't fighting, but she learned more about the truth of trench warfare from what Jack didn't say, and wept when comrades once mentioned frequently were absent in later letters. She read the newspapers too, learning from these what Jack didn't want to tell her, and her dreams were punctured with nightmares of shells, mud and wire. No Man's Land was Dead Man's Land, and Caro's fears for Jack grew with each passing day. He was a man living on borrowed time, and the question was how much would Fate loan him?

Caro knew she appeared every inch the Rector's dutiful daughter, hands often folded demurely in her lap and head bowed presumably in quiet prayer, but beneath this façade her heart was stuttering with terror, and she found it harder to pray with each headline she read. With every list of the fallen her faith ebbed, for it was hard to believe in a benevolent deity when each day even more young men were felled like saplings, their bodies shredded and shattered and sucked into the mud.

How could any kind and loving God approve of such conflict? Caro was sure He couldn't take sides either, for – if she had understood her scriptures sufficiently, and she was intelligent enough to believe she had – He loved everyone regardless of their nationality and their sins. English or German, there was no difference in His eyes, Caro concluded, so there was little point in pleading or trying to make bargains. Instead she sat in the church and held silent conversations with Jack, while the angels with her face danced amid the cherubim. These angels would watch over her, just as the wooden angel Jack had given her last Christmas Eve was always in her pocket and her most precious talisman. Her fingers must stray to it one hundred times a day and each time she sent her heart flying across the restless sea to be with Jack and where it belonged.

I have made your Christmas angel, Jack had written. *I carved her out of a piece of fence post I found – it's hard to believe this mire was once beautiful farmland – and she's a crude thing in comparison to my usual work, yet I find comfort in her. She has your beautiful face and I look upon on her whenever I have a spare minute. She even has a robe made of sacking which I've stitched on – my sewing has earned me a ribbing from the men! I keep your letter folded up inside the secret compartment and I have her close to my heart, carrying your words and your image everywhere I go. She will come home, I promise, for she is our lucky charm. I know that while I have her with me nothing bad can happen. She will protect us.*

It soothed the ache in Caro's heart to think of her letter folded up and hidden inside Jack's new angel. She liked to believe this angel would take care of him when she could not. Heartened, she replied to Jack, conjuring up the Cornish seascape he loved and recalling the story of their love affair and reminding him of their hopes for the future. She would keep their dreams alive, and she was determined to make certain Jack knew he had a wonderful life awaiting him when the war was over and he came home to her. She pictured him in his dugout, reading and rereading her letter before tucking it out of sight in the secret compartment. As she wrote she tried to breathe magic and love and protection into each word and she kissed the paper over and over again, hoping his lips would touch the paper and feel the echo of her lips against his.

The church emptied as she sat lost in thought, the other women leaving as the chill began to bite and the night fell in earnest. She should have been a bride today, laughing and filled with joy, rather than sitting alone in this stone-cold church and aching with loneliness. Her hand rose to her cheeks and she discovered she was weeping, her silent tears falling silently and as incessantly as the young men at the Front. She reached into her pocket for a handkerchief and dabbed her eyes and blew her nose, then rose to her feet. It was time to return to the Rectory and see that Papa ate his dinner. Dwelling on what could have been would not bring Jack home. She had to remain strong for him.

She wondered where Jack was right at this moment. What was Christmas Eve 1914 bringing him? Peace on earth and goodwill to all men? An end to enmity? If she could still pray, Caro would have asked for this. It was what she longed for above all else.

"Bring him home to me," she pleaded, although she wasn't sure quite who she was addressing. Maybe it was the darkening sea and the gathering dusk? Or perhaps, after all, she still wanted to believe in God? Her right hand felt for the ring and turned it again as though making a wish. Maybe one last prayer would be heard, Caro thought, since this was Christmas Eve and the most holy night of them all? She had to try. She had to believe. She needed to believe. She had to believe God heard her.

"Please keep Jack safe. Bring him peace this Christmas and bring him home to me," she whispered, turning to look at the Christ figure on the rood screen. "Keep them all safe this Christmas, German and British, and let there be peace for Christmas."

Above the church the first Christmas Eve stars speared the heavens and Caro's words rose to greet them in a powerful Christmas Eve prayer which, unknown to her, was already being answered in the pockmarked wastes of No Man's Land.

6

Christmas Eve 1914
German Lines
Heinrich

THE NIGHTS WERE WORST. At least by daylight he could see the ravaged landscape of No Man's Land and no matter how ugly the vista at least it was possible to scan the wasteland for a hint of the enemy's position. When the sky was brittle blue and the sun bright the pockmarked land was laid before the exhausted men like an empty beach, with the barbed wire a metallic tideline from which the invaders might choose to press forwards. By day a man could squint against the light and scan the horizon for movement or the tell-tale flash of a bayonet caught in a rogue ray of sunshine. The enemy might choose to advance at any time of night or day, but when the bleak landscape was unveiled by the light you stood a chance of seeing their approach whereas under cover of darkness the enemy could surge forwards, deadly as a rip tide, and the end would be upon you before you had even realised.

Heinrich had lost count of how many nights he'd passed in an agony of listening to the sound of his own breathing while his trembling hand rested on his weapon and his heart crashed against his ribs. His unseeing eyes would strain into the blackness which swirled and reformed into fantastical shapes conjured from his own worst fears and darkest imaginings. On such nights Heinrich pictured himself as a lonesome sentry standing high on a clifftop staring out not over the wastes of No Man's Land but rather an inky ocean while waiting for stealthy invaders to sail closer.

Yes, the nights were worse by far and Heinrich dreaded the times when he had to lead his men out on patrol, creeping through the suffocating darkness to gauge the lie of the land in the sure knowledge that the British would be doing the same. What if they crawled into the enemy, also furtively edging closer, ready to loom from the shadows? Would the next second be his last? Was he prepared to meet his maker? When flares lit the sky goblin green he would drop into the mud and pray they were not betrayed, fingers closing on his pistol and his heart filled with dread. When each excursion was over and they had safely returned, he could barely bring himself to clap his men on the back and congratulate them. He certainly couldn't sit with them to drink coffee by the stove or retell the events of the mission – it was all he could do to collect his writing case and slump at the table to pour his heart out to Heidi.

Heidi. His Heidi. His wife. His heart. His world. Heinrich missed her so much he thought his heart might splinter. Would he ever see her again? Hold her tightly? Kiss her soft lips and breathe in her scent? Trace the J-shaped birth mark on her thigh to make her sigh with pleasure before his hand stole higher? He longed for her in every way, and there wasn't a moment that passed when he didn't wish he had listened to her and stayed at home. If only he'd listened to her when she'd begged him not to enlist. Heidi, who knew him better than he knew himself, had understood that his judgement had been clouded by idealism and had known he would struggle to send another man into eternity, be he never so vile or debased. She had warned him that he was not a man equipped for life as a soldier, and she knew that his imagination and his sensitive nature – the very traits that had driven him to enlist – would render the reality of warfare unbearable to him.

His wife was right; Heinrich was not a natural soldier. His heart raced constantly and his hands trembled so badly he could barely hold a pencil long enough to write to her and say that he was sorry, she had been right all along and he was a teacher not a warrior. His place was in a classroom, drilling children in their alphabet and mathematics, not in France drilling boys with downy upper lips on how to kill young men that in another life they might have played football with or studied alongside. Heidi had understood from the outset that her imaginative husband would struggle with the uncertainty of combat and agonise over the morality of killing men with whom he had no personal grievance and were now deemed the enemy. She had tried to warn him but, with his ears ringing with cries of "For God, Emperor and Empire!", Heinrich hadn't listened. He'd been determined to do his part to defend the Fatherland, and in doing so had ignored the small voice deep inside that had whispered that his wife was right.

"But you're a *teacher*, my love," Heidi had protested, her

amber eyes swimming with tears when Heinrich broke the news that he was considering enlisting. "Let other men fight this war. You're needed here. Your students need you. *I* need you."

But Heinrich, weary of his chalk-dusted gown and airless classrooms, barely heard her choked pleas. His heart was still pounding from the patriotic rhetoric he had been listening to in the town square, and his blood thrummed with a longing to play a part in it all and to make a difference. He *had* to. It was his duty, and nothing anyone said, not even his beloved Heidi, could change his mind. This war was vital to preserving the Empire and their entire way of life, he told her. He *had* to fight. It was his duty. "It's the right thing to do. It's for the Fatherland."

"But not for *you*, my love! You're not a soldier! Please don't do this." Heidi took his hands in hers and pressed them to her cheeks. Heinrich felt the wetness of her tears against his fingers, and his resolve almost broke, for he could never refuse his wife anything. Yet this time he knew there was no choice.

"I'm a patriot," he replied quietly. "I must play my part. Besides, this will be over quickly. The British aren't serious about fighting us. It's just posturing, my love. Everyone says it will all be over by Christmas."

"Truly?" Heidi sounded doubtful.

"Truly. So I'll be home for Christmas," Heinrich insisted, pulling her into his arms.

"You'll be home for Christmas?" Her voice shook and he knew she was trying her hardest to be brave. "You promise?"

Heinrich had hugged her tightly. "Of course, my love. How could I miss your favourite time of the year?"

Heidi adored Christmas, and each festive season the air in

the Schneiders' small townhouse was rich with the scents of cinnamon, nutmeg and oranges. She brought swathes of greenery in from the forest to decorate every inch of the place, gathering it up with red and white ribbons and threading slices of orange and lemon through it. She would bake sugared biscuits to hang on the tree, and even though money was tight, young schoolmasters not earning a huge wage, there was always a small pile of beautifully wrapped presents waiting to be opened on Heiliger Abend – Christmas Eve. One day – soon, they dearly hoped – their own children would come along, and then they would watch the magic of Christmas lighting up their little faces. It was Heidi's dearest wish to become a mother, and a great cause of sadness to them both that they had yet to be blessed with a family.

"You promise to be home for Christmas?" Heidi asked him again, her face pinched with distress, and Heinrich nodded before kissing her tears away. Deep in his heart he knew this was one promise he really shouldn't make, but he couldn't bear to see her distressed.

Today was Christmas Eve and, in spite of his promise and those of the generals, Heinrich was not at home to decorate the tree or light the candles. This broke his heart. The hostilities talked down at the outbreak of the conflict showed no sign of abating – if anything, they appeared to be escalating. Although the German Army held a strong position along the front line and was making steady progress, the British and French had not capitulated as expected, and were even starting to show signs of pushing forward. The winter had proven an unexpected adversary, rain and boots churning the earth into a quagmire before the frost transformed it again into iron, and men shivered in coats that were far too thin for the bitter chill. Seas of mud were frozen into crested oceans with duckboards held fast in ice; walking along them proved treacherous, the slippery planks felling more men than any enemy sharpshooter. There was no scent of gingerbread here, only the stench of death and despair, and rather than boughs of fir trees and slices of orange there were the skeletal remains of the burned trees at the edge of No Man's Land.

Dawn had transformed the ravaged landscape into a sparkling wonderland, and as he sipped bitter coffee, Heinrich reflected on the words of old carols that spoke of bitter winters and iron-hard earth. There was festive beauty to be found even here. After sipping his coffee and smoking the last of his cigarettes, Heinrich settled down to write to Heidi, determined to describe the bleak beauty and the soft chatter of the men as they went about their routine tasks so she could at least share Christmas on paper. He closed his eyes and tried to picture his home with the tree, candles all in place and waiting to be lit at midnight, and the shoes set out for St Nicholas to fill. Heinrich's eyes prickled, and he had to pretend he was coughing in order to account for the sudden rush of tears. Did the British soldiers, still firing guns from somewhere across the mire, also ache for home? He felt certain they must, and it saddened him to think that all of them were so far away from their loved ones and charged with killing one another today of all days. What was this all for? What did all the death achieve? They had moved mere feet in all the months of killing.

As night fell the stars, shy as a girl at her first dance, peeped out from behind wisps of cloud as though making sure the world below was safe to shine upon. Soon hundreds of them freckled the inky sky and Heinrich thought that it must have been on a night like this that angels appeared and sang to shepherds. Heinrich stepped onto the parapet to gaze up at them, and his heart rose to think that Heidi would be looking heavenwards tonight and seeing them too. It made him feel closer to her.

Later, when he looked back on this night, Heinrich could never be certain how the singing began. Was it him who had begun to sing? Or had the carol started further along the line and he had joined in unconsciously? He only knew that the old carol rose up from his soul and he had to sing.

"*Stille Nacht, heilige Nacht. Alles schläft; einsam wacht.*" Heinrich's voice broke a little at the haunting beauty and familiarity of the old carol. Soon the sweet tones of a violin joined in, followed by a flute and more voices as, one by one, the soldiers began to accompany Heinrich's singing. Placing their weapons down, they stepped out of the dugouts and began lighting candles, the shivering flames held aloft and stretching through the gathering night in a trembling necklace of light. As the carols continued, each one celebrating the birth of the Christ child, more soldiers gathered on the ramparts, and soon there were even makeshift Christmas trees fashioned from any remnants of greenery that could be gleaned from the scarred battlefield.

"Merry Christmas!" his men called to each other, and then, to his surprise, they began to call out to the enemy. "Merry Christmas, Tommy! Happy Christmas, English soldiers!"

At first there was no response from the enemy lines. Perhaps they feared this was a trick, which was understandable, Heinrich thought – Greeks and gifts after all – but eventually the good-natured greetings and carols proved irresistible, and answering greetings rang back along with the familiar carols sung in a foreign tongue but no less heartfelt and moving. By unspoken agreement no shells were fired and no patrols ventured out, and when the men on both sides finally retired a deep sense of peace settled over No Man's Land like a feather quilt.

When the sun rose the next morning the world was dusted with a white hoar frost. Heinrich lit a cigarette and smoked thoughtfully, marvelling that for once there was no grumble of artillery or scream of shells but instead a waterfall of birdsong to herald Christmas Day. How long had it been since he had heard birdsong? Heinrich shook his head in wonder that there were even any birds left here. Nature was truly miraculous.

"Sir! Look! There's somebody coming! Is it an attack?"

A soldier at his elbow was pointing into the brightness. Screwing up his eyes against the glare, Heinrich reached for his revolver, but when he saw that the men approaching were waving a flag, seemingly fashioned from underpants, his hand slipped from the holster. Good Lord. Was this really happening?

"No," he said slowly. "I think this is a something else altogether."

He took a deep breath and stepped away from the safety of his own lines into the yawning dangers of No Man's Land, ignoring the shouted warnings from his comrades. If this was a trick then he would soon know about it, Heinrich thought, but this was Christmas Day and he was determined to look for the best in mankind.

Otherwise what had he become? And what was left to fight for?

"Merry Christmas!" A dapper man with a neat moustache stood to attention and held out his hand. "Captain Trevellyn of the First Cornish Rifles! Season's greetings to you, Sir!"

"And to you, Captain!" Heinrich replied, shaking the

outstretched hand rather cautiously. This was, after all, still the enemy, and you couldn't be quite sure. He dredged up his English, fearing it was a little rusty since it was over a decade since he had visited London. "What's all this about?"

"It doesn't seem cricket to shoot at each other today of all days. The chaps wondered if you would be up for a ceasefire," the British captain explained. He nodded towards the British lines, and Heinrich sensed scores of pairs of hopeful eyes trained on him. "We appreciated your impromptu carol concert last night very much. Raised our spirits no end. How about we call a truce just for today, since it's Christmas? It seems a poor show to be fighting today."

"We've brought gifts," added another soldier, brandishing cartons of cigarettes and what looked like a bottle of brandy. Brandy? The British officers clearly had better standards than their German counterparts, Heinrich thought with amusement. Were they playing chess, and off fox-hunting too, when they weren't shelling us?

"Season of goodwill and peace on earth to all men," said Captain Trevellyn. "Even to enemies, what?"

Heinrich could hardly argue with this. As he glanced along the battle lines he realised his opinion didn't even matter, for soldiers on both sides were already moving. As far as the eye could see men from both sides were abandoning their trenches to meet on the frozen land between lines where they shook hands, swapped stories and even began a kickabout with a stuffed hessian sack. Their cries and cheers transported Heinrich back to happier times, looking out at the school playground. How strange and terrible to think that these lads were only a few years older than the children who'd been in his care – and even worse to think that tomorrow they might all be enemies once again. He sighed, digging his chilly hands deep into the pockets of his trench coat, and aware this sense of cold came from far more than the icy wind.

What would Heidi make of this morning's unusual events? Heinrich could hardly wait to sit down and describe it to her in a letter. She would smile and say that this was proof that mankind was intrinsically good. Heidi would remind him that love and friendship would always chase away the darkness, and she would add that this was what the Christmas message was all about. As he watched the men from both sides laugh and smoke and show off pictures of their sweethearts Heinrich prayed that one day he would be at home for Christmas once more, able to share the memory of this most strange celebration with his own children.

He only hoped he would live long enough to have them. He would love a daughter with Heidi's russet hair and amber eyes, and maybe a little boy with his own blond hair and love of books. Clara and Klaus were the names he and Heidi had tentatively given these children, and Heinrich often daydreamed about the happy family life they would lead. There would be a dog, he thought, and wonderful Christmases filled with laughter and Heidi's wonderful cooking. As he pictured this scene now, miles from home and the woman he loved, Heinrich felt a flutter of hope for the first time in months.

"Do you play?" A young British soldier joined Heinrich on the sidelines of the football game. He was tall and had unusual sea-green eyes which danced with good humour and life. The cinnamon sprinkling of freckles across the bridge of his nose and honey tones of his skin betrayed a life spent outside in the sunshine and fresh air, and he brimmed with life and energy.

Heinrich warmed to him straight away. "Sorry?"

The foreign tongue was familiar to him, but Heinrich was little rusty. He had studied English at university but that felt like another life.

The young soldier gestured towards the footballers. "Football? Do you play?"

Heinrich laughed. He was more often found in the library than a playing field. "I'm afraid not. I'm a teacher, so much better at bookwork. You?"

"Badly. I'm more of an artist than a sportsman." He opened a packet of Three Castles and offered Heinrich one. "Want a smoke?"

"*Ja*. Thanks."

Heinrich cupped his hands around the cigarette while the young Tommy struck a match, and they smoked companionably as the players kicked their makeshift ball up and down across the hard earth. Voices yelled and cheered as German and English tongues mingled in the universal language of football. Drawing the smoke into his lungs, Heinrich marvelled how something so normal could be taking place in a world that was anything but. This war was utter madness.

"It feels like a dream," remarked the young man, as though picking up on his thoughts. "Yesterday we were killing one another."

Heinrich flicked the butt of his cigarette onto the frozen ground. Sparks fantailed and fizzled. "Christmas is no time for killing. Neither side has a taste for it today."

The British soldier nodded. "Do any of us ever have a taste for it?"

This was dangerously close to treasonous talk, thought Heinrich. As much as he held the same opinion, it wouldn't do to voice his agreement. He wondered whether his superiors would regret this spontaneous truce. Seeing the enemy as no different to oneself would surely make the men question this war.

If they weren't already doing so ...

Still, it was Christmas and so he held out his hand to the young soldier. "Heinrich," he said.

"Jack," said the young soldier. His handshake was strong and the fingers calloused. A working man, Heinrich surmised, rather than a misplaced intellectual like himself. "A very merry Christmas to you, Jack," he said as they shook hands.

"And to you too, Sir," the young man replied. "This is a turn-up for the books, isn't it?"

Heinrich frowned and glanced about. "There are books?"

"Sorry. It's a saying. It means a situation is unusual."

"Ah." Heinrich understood now. "Indeed yes, today is most unusual. Yet in another lifetime it would not be so strange, I think, for Germans and British to be friends. In my youth I spent a very happy few months in London. It's a beautiful city, almost as lovely as Hamburg."

Jack looked wistful. "I hope to see them both for myself one day. I haven't travelled far from home yet. To tell the truth, I hadn't even left Cornwall until I came here."

"Well, you're younger than me," Heinrich said kindly, although they both knew this wasn't the reason a man like Jack had not ventured far from his place of birth. "Once this is all over you'll be able to see the world for yourself."

"I hope so," Jack said but his voice was taut with sadness. It seemed to Heinrich that this lad doubted he would live to see the New Year, let alone visit the most beautiful cities in Europe, and Heinrich hated seeing such resignation. The teacher in him wanted to give this young man hope that his dreams would come true.

"This is not for ever, my friend," he told Jack. "One day this will just be history, and people will scratch their heads when they try to understand what it was all about. Maybe we will meet at a pavement café in Paris. Or perhaps our children will be friends. Empires rise and fall. It is the way of things."

"Do you think so?" Jack asked, as eagerly as a child asking a parent for reassurance that a night terror was no more than a bad dream.

"Indeed. History teaches us this, and by looking back we see the future," Heinrich said, closing the matter neatly, as he so often had in his classroom. How he missed his students. Would he ever teach again? Would he stand in a classroom describing this strange meeting? Or would Jack's bullet fell him in the morning? He shivered and huddled deeper into his coat.

Sobered by this downwards trajectory in his mood, he turned the conversation to their lives away from the war. Jack lit two more cigarettes and as they smoked he described the quiet coastal part of England that was his home, said proudly that he was engaged to be married to the most wonderful girl in the world, and explained that he fostered aspirations of becoming a sculptor. Although he was younger than Heinrich by at least a decade there was something about his determination to make his fiancée proud that reminded Heinrich of himself. If he'd had Jack in his class, he would have done all he could to help this young man better himself. He would have guided him and found a way to help him fulfil his ambition to travel. But this time tomorrow he might well be duty bound to call this lad an enemy and do his utmost to kill him.

All that energy and potential and life would be cut down in its prime, and for what? He had no desire to kill young boys like this. Hadn't his sole purpose been to nurture them and help them become adults capable of building a better world? Was this what it meant to be a patriot, to kill young boys with their whole lives ahead of them?

"Jack! We need you over here! Fritz is licking us!" Two soldiers, red-faced and panting from their exertions on the improvised pitch, were waving to Jack.

"You had best join in," Heinrich said. "Your nation's honour is at stake."

Jack grimaced. "I'm so useless I'll be the enemy's secret weapon. Still, can't let the side down. Merry Christmas, Heinrich."

"Merry Christmas, Jack," he replied quietly. "And the very best of luck."

They both knew he wasn't referring to the football match, and for a moment the bright winter sunshine seemed to dim and the blue sky was a little less bright.

"And to you too, Sir," said Jack, and they clasped hands once more, each knowing that tomorrow the landscape would be very different. "A very merry Christmas."

He sprinted away, laughing and jostling with lads on both sides – and something fell from his pocket, bouncing across iron hard ridges of mud like a ball.

"You've dropped something!" Heinrich called after him. "Jack! Wait a moment!"

But there was far too much noise coming from the excited players, and Heinrich's call was swallowed up by whoops and cheers. He shielded his eyes against the brightness of the low sun, hoping to catch sight of his new friend, but it was impossible to distinguish one khaki-clad form from another as more and more young men joined in. Moving as one, the mass twisted and surged away from the German camp and towards the front line until it was hard to tell which soldiers belonged to which side.

Heinrich retrieved the object which had slipped from the young man's jacket, surprised to discover it was a carved angel. Fashioned from rough fence wood and cobbled together with materials gleaned from trench life, he guessed it was a talisman and no less precious for its humble origins. At the Front men became superstitious, clinging to whatever hope and charms they believed might keep them alive, and even a staunch Lutheran like Heinrich would find himself embracing odd rituals. His picture of Heidi, taken in the Berlin studio for her seventeenth birthday, was his own lucky charm, and he would press his lips to the image each night and pray that he would see her again. Each kiss bought him an extra day – if he forgot, who knew what might happen?

Heinrich scanned the wastes again, hoping to catch sight of the young soldier, but Jack had vanished into a sea of grey and khaki. Shaking his head, Heinrich studied the angel and was taken back by the beauty of the piece. The materials might be crude but the craftsmanship was undeniable.

The English soldier was a talented sculptor.

Heinrich tucked the angel into his breast pocket, fully intending to search for the young soldier, but he was interrupted by a group of officers, keen to wish him Merry Christmas and share cognac. There was singing and more cognac and even a plum pudding, and soon the light was fading. The British officers shook hands and headed back to their own trenches. The football teams had been disbanded.

Heinrich scanned the emptying wasteland for Jack, but there was no sign of the young English soldier. The strange

Christmas Day gathering was ending as quickly as it had begun and, however unintentionally, it seemed that the carved angel had swapped sides. Heinrich hoped that Jack wasn't too upset by its loss. He ran his forefinger over the sweet features, and was surprised to find a comfort in the thought of it watching over him now, an idea which made him choke out a bitter laugh. What help could a wooden angel be, since even the heavenly ones had turned their faces away from mankind? It would take more than that to protect anyone from the carnage of this godforsaken war.

But Heinrich Schneider was mistaken; Jack's angel was to prove more powerful than he could have ever imagined. Two days later, when the Christmas truce had the semblance of a very strange dream and the guns were coughing death once more, Heinrich's outpost was ambushed by the enemy. Asleep and unprepared, only the wooden trunk of the carved angel, still nestled in the breast pocket of his coat, stood between the viper strike of a bayonet blade and Heinrich's heart when the enemy's blade slashed through his upstretched arm and into his chest.

The carved angel had taken the blow that should have ended Heinrich Schneider's life. If he hadn't picked her up and kept her safe he would have died in a dugout, miles from home and far away from his beloved Heidi.

The angel had saved his life.

"Someone's watching over you," was the MO's comment when Heinrich arrived in the field hospital. "If that blade had reached its target you'd have been in the meat wagon."

Heinrich's trembling left hand curled around the angel. The angel's trunk was damaged but the tightly stitched robe remained miraculously intact and her serene and beautiful face showed no trace of the violence done to her wooden person. He owed his life to the work of an English lad called Jack, and as he lay in the hospital bed Heinrich knew he would be thankful for this angel for the rest of his life – a life she had saved and which he now felt certain would be long and happy. He would be invalided home now, and for him at least the war was over.

Heinrich Schneider owed *everything* to Jack's lost angel and to the talented young man who'd crafted her.

7

The present
London
Ellen

"AND YOU FOUND that letter inside your gran's decoration?"

Anna was thrown when, having popped over on the off-chance of persuading Ellen to venture out to a party, she found her best friend holding a yellowed scrap of paper and blotting her eyes with a sodden tissue. Ellen's voice was shaky as she hiccupped out the story of a girl called Caro who had loved a boy called Jack, waved him off to war and broke her heart missing him. Ellen was so upset that it took a while for Anna to realise all these events had taken place over a century ago and to people long since gone.

"A carpenter called Jack carved this angel for his fiancée, Caro." Ellen passed the angel to Anna. "She's hollow inside, see? He made one like it earlier to hold her engagement ring, and promised to make another angel every year for the rest of his life. Isn't that romantic?"

"Just a bit. Most of my exes thought they'd done well to pick up some flowers from the Shell garage! Maybe men were more romantic back then?"

"Maybe," said Ellen, dabbing her eyes again. "The way she wrote to him is definitely romantic. She reminded him how they'd first met, their first kiss, how she longed to be married and make love to him properly, their dreams of travelling. I felt quite voyeuristic reading her letter."

"She must have died years ago," Anna pointed out gently.

"I know that logically, but it's as if the things she writes about happened only days ago. Honestly, Caro Sweethouse could walk past right now – that's how real this all feels. Why don't you read her letter and see for yourself? I'll make us some tea."

"Sod tea. I'll need a gin if I'm going to end up a sobbing mess like you," Anna replied, tucking her legs underneath her and nestling into the sofa.

By the time she had finished reading the stars were venturing out for the night and the streetlights were on. She put the page down on the arm of the sofa and smoothed it with her hand. "My goodness. I can see why reading that made you cry. Her words are beautiful, aren't they? She really adored him."

Ellen nodded. "I love how he hid her letter inside the angel for safe keeping. It feels as though she's been watching over their love story ever since."

"She certainly has, and now we know about it they aren't forgotten." Anna turned the angel upside down, marvelling at the intricate mechanism which concealed the hiding place. "Goodness, that was so clever. Nobody would have a clue unless they stripped away the hessian tunic and looked really closely."

"The way she wrote to him is so eloquent," Ellen said wistfully. "It makes you believe in true love, doesn't it?"

"You sound like your granny. You'll be talking about signs and true love next," Anna teased.

Ellen stared at her friend.

He'll be your angel. Look for a sign.

Surely not? It was just a silly coincidence, but even so shivers dusted her skin.

"I wish somebody would write to me like that," Anna continued. "I must have been born in the wrong century. Swiping right just isn't the same, is it? And can you imagine a guy being happy to wait for sex until you were married, and being content to hold your hand instead?"

"I'm not sure Jack or Caro were *content* with hand-holding. She seemed pretty keen for their wedding night to arrive," pointed out Ellen. The longing for Jack's touch, held across the years by Caro's slanting hand, made her own heart yearn for more.

"Well, Jack sounds like he was a gentleman, and there's few of them about these days. Did I tell you about the last date I went on, with the hot guy from the coffee shop? He only told me I could pay for dinner because I'm an accountant and earn more than him!"

"Who says romance is dead?"

"As a dodo in his case. I didn't mind paying, because I *do* earn more. It was the assumption that I would have to – trust me, that wasn't attractive. Suddenly he didn't seem nearly as hot."

"What did you do?"

"After the main course was over I pretended a family

matter had come up. It was worth paying to escape! I'll be avoiding Starbucks on the High Street from now on."

"Costa it is," Ellen said.

"Yep." Anna looked thoughtful. "I bet Jack treated Caro like a lady. Even though he was 'just' a carpenter he sounds like a gentleman. God, listen to me! I sound half in love with him myself."

"Join the club. Anyway, for what it's worth I don't think their stations mattered to them in the slightest. They were determined to be together. From what Caro wrote they defied everyone to become a couple. She says her father wasn't exactly thrilled."

"Very Romeo and Juliet," Anna agreed. "They had so many plans for the future, but then the war came and who knows what happened then? I guess the chances are Jack never made it home. Not many men did, from what I can recall from my GCSEs."

Ellen recalled the English lessons the two friends had shared a lifetime ago in airless classrooms where boys swung on their chairs and did their best to attract the girls' attention while teachers fought with whiteboards and struggled to interest teenagers in pararhyme and extended metaphors. She remembered being moved by the stories of Wilfred Owen trudging through the mud, Kit Rivers pulling torn comrades from the barbed wire, and Rupert Brooke becoming forever England in an alien plot of land – but these details, although tragic, seemed remote when viewed through the prism of history. Now she had glimpsed the Great War through the eyes of Caro Sweethouse the same texts felt unbearably immediate and real.

"I hate to think Jack lost the angel. Caro loved knowing he

was keeping her letter inside it," she said quietly. "She had hoped to hold it, and Jack, by Christmas."

"When they said the war would be over by then," Anna remembered, "they really got that wrong."

"I know. I can't bear to think what they went through," Ellen said with a wobble in her voice. She pushed her russet curls behind her ears and sniffed. "Waiting at home for news must have been awful. Poor Caro."

Anna was moved by what she had read, but she was surprised by how upset her Ellen was. Her friend hadn't been this vocal when her own relationship ended. The century-old love story had really touched her heart, and Anna was relieved to discover Ellen did still believe in love for, like Clara, Anna knew her lovely friend was too special to shut her heart away.

"And the angel belonged to your great-grandfather? The German one?" she asked quickly, not wanting Ellen to cry again.

Ellen nodded. "According to Mum he bought it back from the Front. He treasured it, and she thinks there was some story about it saving his life, but that could just be a family myth."

Anna's forehead pleated. "But how would a *German* soldier, the enemy, come across Jack's angel? And how could a small Christmas decoration like that save anyone's life?"

Ellen wished she knew the answers to these questions. She wished even more that she had thought to ask Clara more about her family and the past while she had still been alive. How sad that so many stories were lost in time. The little anecdotes and tales that build a picture of who we are and what make us are far too easily lost. Had Great-grandpa Heinrich found the angel on the battlefield? Or had he killed

Jack in battle and taken the angel as a trophy? War did strange things to people.

She shuddered. Surely her own great-grandfather wouldn't have done something so repellent? Heinrich Schneider had been, by all accounts, a gentle soul and a respected schoolteacher who had lived quietly in Hamburg and devoted his life to education. Then again war wasn't black and white, no matter what Hollywood might insist. Who could say what Heinrich Schneider might have done when fighting for his life, or what anyone might do to survive?

Troubled, Ellen picked up the angel. She felt sure that her great-grandfather had kept this angel not as a trophy but because it had meant something very special to him. There was more to the lost angel's story. She knew there was.

"I don't suppose we'll ever know the reason why he had it. It's a mystery," she sighed.

The reality of all the lost stories, the precious memories melted like snow in sunlight, and the cherished mementoes rendered meaningless by the passing years made Ellen's heart ache. It felt unbearably final that Jack and Caro and Heinrich were long gone and the answers lost with them. Who was left to remember them now, apart from the little angel? If only she could speak.

"You said your mum thought the angel saved his life, which was why he kept hold of it. Your granny kept her too, so there must be something in that story," Anna pointed out.

"Granny was a hoarder. Mum did say that she was upset when she couldn't find it after she had cleared her parents' house in Germany. I wish I'd thought to ask her more about her family when I had the chance, but it all seemed so long ago."

"It *was* a long time ago."

Anna took the angel and turned her around slowly. "That gash in the wood looks like it could have been made by the tip of a blade. What do you think?"

"It's possible. Mum thinks her cousin Sabine might know something – not that we're in touch with her very often. She said she'd ask."

"Don't forget Ancestry," suggested Anna. "And Facebook's always good for a stalk. I find out lots of things that way."

"Mostly about your exes," Ellen laughed. "You're a stalker!"

Anna grinned. "Guilty as charged – but I bet they stalk me too, which is why I never allow any fat pictures online! Anyway, never mind my exes, here's a thought for you – if it *was* the case that the angel saved your great-grandfather's life, then if not for her you wouldn't be here at all. None of your family would. How's that for blowing your mind?"

This was an enormous concept and Ellen was lost for words. That this small wooden angel could have changed her own destiny was some leap of imagination, and yet something about the theory rang true. Life was often balanced on small and seemingly meaningless decisions. A route chosen. A party attended. A bus missed. These were all sliding-door moments, points in time where one possible life slipped away and another slotted into place. So why shouldn't the lost angel have played a pivotal role in her own destiny?

"Maybe that's true," she said slowly. "Granny Clara also said she was sending me a guardian angel."

"Job done," said Anna.

"Half a job. She said she was sending her guardian angel to help me find the love of my life. She was obsessed with people finding love."

"She must have been the only nonagenarian who watched Love Island!"

Anna had been surprised, and secretly rather impressed, when visiting Clara one evening to discover the elderly lady glued to the antics of a pool full of scantily clad twenty-somethings.

"I wasn't always old," Clara laughed, seeing Anna's raised eyebrows. "We did have sex back in my day, you know!"

Anna hadn't known quite what to say. Ellen's sweet old grandmother was supposed to talk about knitting and watch Songs of Praise.

"Granny, stop it!" Ellen scolded, muting the television and earning a glare from Clara, who was following a heated argument between two girls who were both after a perma-tanned hunk. "You're embarrassing Anna."

"I'm German, so I can be blunt," Clara said tartly, reaching for the remote and turning the sound back up. "And I'm old too, which means I can put enjoying watching such rubbish down to being gaga rather than being lowbrow, unlike you youngsters. What's *your* excuse, hmm?"

The memory of Clara made the girls smile. She had been a force of nature..

"Love Island isn't romantic," pointed out Ellen, who was still thinking about Jack and Caro and the sweetness of her letter. "Jack and Caro were so in love, and her letter was really romantic. I bet his would have been, too. I wonder if he made it home to marry her?"

"Why don't we find out?" Anna suggested.

"Write to the War Graves people, you mean? See if they can trace a Jack Tregenna?"

"That's one possibility, but I imagine it might take a while to hear back. No, I had a more immediate solution in mind. What are you doing tomorrow? Anything planned?"

Ellen laughed. "You know my social calendar's empty."

Anna picked up Caro's letter and pointed to the top right-hand corner where a faded yet still elegant hand had written the sender's address: *The Rectory, Church Lane, Penmarloe.*

"Time to take a trip to Cornwall," she said.

8

The present
December
Penmarloe
Ellen

ANNA'S FIAT 500 turned the final bend of a steep lane threaded through hills folded like double cream. After a long drive night had eventually yawned into morning and as the girls marvelled at the steep valley and the cluster of cottages clinging to its sides like ivy-packaged parcels, a fat red sun was hauling itself behind them up into a sealskin sky, turning the frost sprinkled over the frozen world into a thousand fallen stars. Every branch sparkled, smoke drifted lazily from chimney pots and in the distance the sea was a liquid gold line against a peach sky.

Wintry Cornwall was a world away from London. Maybe this peninsula was more of a state of mind than a location, and a place where magic was possible, for it seemed to Ellen that the closer the car drew to Penmarloe the wider the angel's smile grew. Perhaps she knew she was coming home to return Caro's love letter to the place where it had been penned? Such a magical feat seemed more than possible in this enchanted landscape of steep and narrow lanes, moorland, deep coombes and ancient Celtic crosses.

As dawn's pink ribbons threaded the sky Ellen knew the distance between this place and London was greater than the physical miles, and it was as though in taking Anna up on her offer of a spontaneous road trip west she'd left one version of herself behind and adopted another entirely. This Ellen was stepping into the unknown and embracing the possibility of change, shrugging off logic and routine, and listening to the conviction that this was where she was meant to be. She wasn't certain whether she believed in ghosts, but she had the oddest feeling that Clara, not far away, was nodding her approval.

Look for a sign.

Was this sign the lost angel?

There are points in life where pathways fork and new directions beckon. As Anna had outlined her plan for a trip west to Cornish village where Caro and Jack had lived at the turn of the last century, Ellen knew that visiting Penmarloe would change everything. She might find out things about her great-grandfather, unpleasant details of his conduct in battle, that could never be unlearned. How might she view herself and her heritage then? Or perhaps they would find nothing at all, Caro and Jack's story swallowed up by the passing of the years with no trace left of the vibrant young people they'd been. Jack had in all likelihood died in France, like so many others of that lost generation, remembered only each November with poppies and poetry. The journey westwards was a liminal space between the present Ellen and the future one. Who would that girl be? And what did the hours ahead hold in store?

"Why would we go to Cornwall now?" Ellen had asked, surprised by Anna's suggestion. "It's the middle of winter. Hardly the right time for surfing."

"With a wetsuit it's a great time to surf," Anna countered. "But that's not the point of the trip. Let's head to where Caro lived in 1914 and see if we can find anything out about her. We've got the address from the letter, so that's a starting place."

"But it was such a long time ago. Nobody will remember her now," Ellen sighed.

Anna raised her eyes to the ceiling. "Stop being such a pessimist. We might find something out from the parish records or gravestones. Wouldn't it be brilliant if we could answer some questions? And if it's a wild goose chase, so what? Cornwall in the winter is brilliant. Log fires, long walks on deserted beaches and cosy pubs with piles of food – what's not to like?"

"But Christmas is in a under a week's time."

"Says the girl who hasn't even bought a tree? Come on, give me one good reason why we shouldn't just take off like Thelma and Louise? Without the Grand Canyon bit, obviously! Come on Ellen, live a little! Life is short!"

Live a little. Life is short.

Ellen looked up, jolted. These were words she had heard Clara utter many times. A born worrier, Ellen fretted about taking a chance on many things from going on a date to accepting a job to splurging a week's wages on a pair of beautiful shoes. *Live a little,* Clara would urge her. *Life is short!* Her grandmother had lived by this philosophy right until the very end, and now, hearing the words again, Ellen felt as though Clara was sitting in the flat and wagging her finger at her.

A decade before, widowed and missing her husband terribly, Clara North had shocked her family by deciding to travel around Europe alone. Harry wasn't coming back, she explained with a catch in her voice. Her beloved husband had gone to a place she couldn't yet follow, and no amount of weeping or refusing to get out of bed would bring him back. Yes, she missed him dreadfully, but she knew her husband, a pragmatic man, would have been furious if she gave in to grief. Life was short – she realised this more than ever – and it was time to live a little in whatever time she had left.

Ignoring the worries of her daughter, Clara booked herself onto the Eurostar and headed off for six months to see Rome and Venice and dozens of other places she had dreamed of visiting. Bitten hard by the travel bug, she had gone on to enjoy adventures all over the globe, and even a few months before her death had been planning an excursion to Peru. In Clara's case, 'live a little' was more like 'live a lot'.

Ellen knew her grandmother would have leapt at the chance of an unexpected jaunt to Cornwall. She'd have been in the car already and revving the engine, desperate to find out who Jack and Caro were and how her father had come to have their angel. Maybe it was time Ellen took her grandmother's advice and lived a little?

Or even lived a lot?

"Okay," she had said. "Why not?"

Anna punched the air. "Cornwall, here we come! Go and pack your toothbrush!"

She was on Airbnb before Ellen was out of the room, and

by time she had returned with an overnight bag the girls were booked into a tiny fisherman's store on the harbour side.

"Last-minute availability," Anna said triumphantly, beckoning Ellen over and scrolling through pictures of a cosy beam-ceilinged bedsit, filled with squashy sofas and fairy lights, and with a cheerful logburner glowing in the corner. "We're lucky to find this so close to Christmas. Somebody up there wants us to visit! Maybe it's your granny?"

"Maybe," laughed Ellen. "Or perhaps you scrolled through twenty booked places first?"

"You cynic! This was the first one I came across. As I said, you're meant to go to Cornwall. I can feel it!"

After a flying visit to Anna's house to collect her overnight things, the two had set off on their road trip, singing loudly to cheesy Christmas music, feeling excited at the unexpected adventure. The journey west was smooth, the late-night motorway practically deserted, and Ellen was so busy researching the area they were visiting that the time flew by. Having never visited Cornwall before she could hardly wait to see it for herself.

According to the Southwest Tourist Board, Penmarloe claimed to be the most picturesque fishing village in Cornwall, and as Anna drove westwards Ellen scrolled through pages of picture-postcard views of whitewashed cottages, primary-coloured fishing boats and a granite harbour. Although the look of the place must have changed little since Jack and Caro's time, the cluster of boutique hotels overlooking the beach, the six-figure property prices on Rightmove and the presence of a Michelin starred fish restaurant hinted that many changes lay behind the lime-washed walls. These cobbled streets were no longer trodden by hobnailed work boots but by colourful wellies and designer deck shoes.

Would Jack's carpenter's shop be a holiday let now? Caro's descriptions were so vivid, with its low door and deep roof, that Ellen could almost smell the curls of wood carpeting the earth floor and see the sawdust floating in the air.

"Breakfast first, or exploring?" Anna asked once they had parked and were walking into the village. She tucked her arm through Ellen's. "I'm dying for a fry-up."

But Ellen was too excited to eat. The air was salty on her lips and the light clear and sharp, and everywhere she looked were breathtaking views. Caro had seen these hills and had walked Bramble along these narrow streets. The scenes from the letter, already clear in Ellen's mind, were even more so now. Caro and Jack might wander past at any moment.

"Exploring," Ellen said firmly. Then she gasped. "Oh my goodness! There's the church where Caro's father was the Rector!"

"Let's start there, then," said Anna.

A grey crenellated tower peeped out between the bare branches of sycamores and chestnuts, as coy as a teenager peeking through a straggly fringe. A low wall, lichen-furred and crumbly as fudge, set the church apart from the lane. Old stones, listing drunkenly at the heads of mounds as gently plumped as feather duvets, bore the carved names blurred by years of relentless Cornish storms. St Julietta's. The place where Jack had proposed to Caro, and the church which housed the rood screen topped with angels he had carved with such love and devotion.

The Rectory was adjacent to the church and in true Jane Austen style was a large Queen Anne building complete with sweeping lawns, large sashed windows and an immaculate gravelled drive. A large Christmas tree stood in the middle of the turning circle, and the neatly clipped hedges were decorated with jaunty red bows and white lights. It was a beautiful house, square and solid, and imbued with years of status and dignity. Standing beside twin pillars which guarded the entrance like granite sentries, Ellen felt quite intimidated by the grandeur. This was a house which oozed status and served as a reminder to all who saw it of their own place in the world. How nervous Jack must have felt when he called here, cap in hand, to ask the Reverend Sweethouse for his daughter's hand in marriage.

"It's a beautiful house, isn't it?" A woman with two spaniels at her heels had stopped alongside the gate to join Ellen and Anna in their admiration of the elegant building. The dogs jumped up at Anna, barking delightedly, and their owner tugged them back with an eye roll.

"Get down with your filthy paws! Oh! I'm so sorry! You bad dogs!"

"Don't worry. They're fine," Ellen said, crouching down to pet them. But Anna, fearing muddy paw prints on her white jeans, stepped backwards hastily.

"They are *not* fine," sighed the owner, doing her best to reel the dogs in. "I'm afraid they have absolutely no manners. Down Adam! Down Eve! You'd think a vicar's dogs would be far more godly, wouldn't you? They must have been sent so I could work on my patience."

Although she was burrowed inside a Puffa jacket, a crisp white clerical collar poked above the collar. She must be the twenty-first century successor to Caro's father, thought Ellen. How was this meeting for another sign?

"Are you the vicar here?" she asked.

"Guilty as charged! I'm Reverend Beverley Jones, or Bev the Rev to the people of the village – what's left of them these days."

"Do you live in there?" Anna was impressed.

But the Reverend Beverley laughed. "In my dreams! The C of E sold these kinds of places off long ago. Churches aren't cheap to run, and every penny counts these days. Today's vicarage is a new build at the top of the village. It's nowhere near as grand, but it has central heating and insulation, so I count my blessings. This place must cost a fortune to heat."

Ellen was disappointed, but what had she hoped for. A tour? The Reverend Sweethouse to somehow be in situ? Of course a such a beautiful house had been sold. It was a reminder that the world had truly moved on since 1914.

"Who lives here now?" she asked, peering down the drive where a Bentley and a new Range Rover cuddled up by the sweeping flight of stone steps. She wondered if she was brave enough to knock on the door and ask for a tour.

The vicar shrugged. "I'm not sure. It's a holiday home like most of the other houses in the village. It's the same for most of the houses in the heart of the village."

"A Reverend Sweethouse lived here once. I've come across a letter that belonged to his daughter." Ellen wasn't sure why she blurted this out to Bev. Maybe it was a confessional thing?

"Goodness, that must have been a very long time ago," said Bev the Rev, while the spaniels twirled around her as though she was a Puffa-clad maypole. Once untangled she added, "I've seen his name on the roll in the church. That was in the nineteen hundreds, I think? First World War time."

"That's him. He had a daughter called Caroline." Ellen's hand slid into her pocket and brushed against the angel. "I've found a letter she wrote to her fiancé, who was away at the Front. I was wondering what happened to her."

"She would have died a long time ago, of course," said Bev

the Rev, "but she might be buried here. There's a plan of the graves somewhere. What was her name?"

"Caroline Sweethouse. She was engaged to the village carpenter, Jack Tregenna."

"Tregenna? That's a local name, all right. There's lots of Tregennas in the graveyard. You could ask up at Sea Angel too and see what they know."

"Sea *Angel*?" Ellen glanced at Anna. How many more signs could there be?

"It's the last house before the cliff path – you can't miss it. The Tregenna family lives there. They can tell you more about John Tregenna, too." Bev said this name as though it should mean something.

"John Tregenna?" Ellen echoed. "Who was John Tregenna?"

"The sculptor!" Bev regarded Ellen with surprise. "Isn't that who you meant?"

"Jack's the name I have. He wanted to be a sculptor. He was carving the rood screen."

"*John* Tregenna carved the rood screen in our church. Adam! Eve! Will you stop that?" The dogs bungeed on their leads and Bev yanked at them half-heartedly.

"John Tregenna made the rood screen here?" Ellen pressed, so intent on what Bev was telling her that she barely noticed the canine macrame wound around her ankles. It had to be the same person. Did this mean Jack had survived the war and become a sculptor after all? Dare she hope that there had been a happy ending?

"That's right," said Bev. "He was quite successful, I believe, and those in the know seem to like his work. Makes our screen a headache to insure. Could they be the same person?

This John and your Jack? Jack's sometimes an informal name for John, isn't it?"

Ellen nodded slowly. "It's possible. Caro writes about the rood screen in the village church because she felt closer to Jack whenever she looked at it. He was away fighting at the Front, and she lived in terror of bad news."

"It must have been a dreadful time," said Bev, shaking her head. "I don't recall reading Jack's name out when we do the roll of honour in November, so I'd put money on it being the same guy making it through against all the odds. Not that I'm a betting woman, of course! How incredible if you have a letter that was his. You never know, it could be worth something. The people at the Cornish Heritage Trust might be able to help you find out more. They're based at Rosecraddick Manor, just up the road."

"Isn't that the Kit Rivers place?" Anna asked excitedly. "I saw the film about him a while back. It made me bawl my eyes out."

Ellen had seen it too, and been swept away by the romance of a lost love, secret diaries and the story of a young man doomed to remain forever twenty-two, sepia-frozen in his dashing captain's uniform. Could Caro and Jack have been a small part of that tale? She felt sure they must.

"That's right," said Bev. "I won't lie – the film has brought a fair amount of tourism to the area, which has to be a good thing. Penhayes is very popular, too, with all the literary connections and the artists. The Rosecraddick Set is what they're calling those young men now. We don't get quite as much attention here, because people are far more excited about tragic love affairs than religious iconography. The rood screen is considered interesting because it's Tregenna's earliest known work, in wood not stone, but it's not exactly a moneyspinner for the village. It's beautiful, though, and it's covered in––"

"Angels," interrupted Ellen. Of course it was. She slid the lost angel from her pocket and balanced it on the palm of her hand. Was it imagination or was the sweet smile wider still, as though the angel was enjoying the reveal? "I imagine the ones in the church look a bit like this one?"

Bev's eyes were saucers. "I'll say they do! That angel is *identical!*"

"So you think she could have been carved by the same man?" Ellen asked, although she already knew the answer.

"I'll eat my dog collar if she wasn't. But don't take my word for it. Come and see for yourselves! And if that is a Tregenna piece ..." Bev the Rev exhaled and shook her head. "Well, then I'd get it insured pronto, because it's something very special."

Ellen nodded. Bev was right. The angel was special. She was more than special.

She was priceless.

9

December 1914
The Western Front
Jack

"ARE YOU ALL RIGHT, JACK?"

Jack glanced up from rifling through his pockets. His friend Alex Evans, box brownie camera held loosely in his hand, was standing in the doorway of the dugout and regarding him with great concern. Straightening up, Jack raked a shaking hand through his hair.

"I can't find the angel I carved for Caro."

He knew Alex would understand his distress. The two men had enlisted at the same time and, like Jack, Alex had stood on the deck of the ship which bore the new recruits to France and wondered whether he would ever see the vanishing shoreline and his beloved again. He knew that thoughts of sweethearts and home were all that kept a man from sinking into madness here on the Front.

"It could have slipped under the pallet?" he suggested. "Or got caught up in your blanket roll?"

"I've looked there," said Jack miserably, scrabbling beneath his pallet for the umpteenth time. The dugout was scooped out of the side of a trench and had scarcely room to house the six men quartered inside. There was nowhere for anything to be hidden.

"Maybe one of the other chaps has hidden her as a joke?" Alex suggested

It was unlikely; each man here knew exactly what letters and mementoes from home meant. The soldiers were a superstitious bunch, too, and all understood how here items took on new meanings and became imbued with powers way beyond the ordinary. At the Front insignificant objects became lucky charms that could keep a man alive and draw him safely home again. To lose such a talisman was to lose hope and any remaining grasp on the fraying threads of sanity. Jack knew no soldier would want to inflict such cruel suffering on a comrade.

Alex began searching beneath the small table where the men sat to write letters and play cards, but to no avail. The angel had vanished.

"I've lost her," Jack said. "I must have dropped her in No Man's Land when we were playing football."

"I'm really sorry, pal," said Alex, resting a hand on his shoulder. "I wish I could help."

Jack choked out his thanks and headed outside into the trench. With a shaking hand he lit a cigarette in a desperate attempt to calm himself, but even as he drew the smoke into his lungs he already knew this was futile. His heart was racing and his throat was closing with a suffocating dread he'd never encountered before – not even when faced with shells and gunfire. His angel was lost. Caro's precious letter, the record of their love story to date, was gone. His talisman was missing, and Jack knew that from now on his life would be counted in days or even hours.

When the order to advance came Jack always managed to lock terror up in a place where thought and imagination couldn't find it. This was the only way he could cope with the long interludes of inertia punctuated with violent and soul-shredding terror. Jack had come to understand very early on that if he allowed himself to let fear rule his heart he would never rouse himself from his bunk, let alone pick up a weapon to kill men he had no argument with – men like the kindly schoolteacher Heinrich with his sad eyes and wise words. Yet if Jack didn't shoot them these men would undoubtedly kill him, if not today or tomorrow then very soon. How could anyone cling onto their sanity in such a world?

Each man found his own way to cope. Some soldiers smoked. Others drank rough French beer in the taverns near the towns where they were billeted, amusing themselves with the local girls or playing dice and a few, like Jack's commanding officer, who in another life had been Kit Rivers from the manor, spent hours composing poetry. Jack chose to lose himself in carving, the passion of the past becoming a panacea for the horrors of the present, and with each stroke of his knife he thought of Caro, and with each curl of shaved wood that drifted down to the mud he sent his love flying across the grey sea to Penmarloe. With only the crudest pieces of wood Jack could still create elaborate wild creatures. For fun he even carved a likeness of the beady-eyed rat which one of the men had tamed and christened Kitchener.

Jack's work attracted admiration, and before long he was

taking commissions. He made a crucifix for one young man who hoped to become a priest once the war was over, and whittled countless carvings of dogs and horses, even a daisy requested by Captain Rivers. The men were baffled by this, but Jack thought he understood and was glad to be able to offer his commanding officer this small comfort.

To lose his own comfort was unbearable. Jack felt as though the floor of the trench had given way beneath his boots, plunging him deeper and deeper into the horror. Without the angel, the first of the Christmas angels he'd promised to give Caro, he was alone and abandoned. He was unprotected. While she was in his possession Jack knew he would stay alive because he had promised to return home to give her to Caro. Jack would never break a promise made to the woman he loved, and although it was superstitious he knew that while he had the angel in his possession he would stay safe. But without her?

Without her, Jack would never see his beloved Caro again.

The angel was more than Jack's talisman; she was also the keeper of Caro's cherished words. When he was at his lowest ebb Jack would cut the stitches open and re-read each beloved line. Then and only then would he allow his thoughts to fly across the cratered wastelands, over the water and back home to Cornwall and the girl he loved. He would press the paper to his lips, comforted by the knowledge it held the echo of her touch. He hoped she knew that each letter he sent to her was covered in kisses and that his love flowed through the ink and grew with each scratch of nib on paper.

Would he ever know Caro's touch again? Jack fretted when the darkness closed in and another shell lit up the darkness and made the earth buck beneath his feet. Would he hold her again? Press his mouth against the softness of her hair? See her eyes light up when she saw him? Hear her laughter ring out at Bramble's antics? Kiss her? Ever make love to her? Would he live to marry her and hold their children, falling in love with her all over again as he saw their joy recreated in each new face? Would they visit Florence and Rome? Cross the ocean to America? Grow old together? Or would he die here in the mud and be buried beneath alien soil? Would anyone even know where he fell? Would Caro be doomed to wonder where he was and what had become of him? That idea broke his heart, and he doubled his resolve to survive.

Jack had to believe that all the things he longed for would come to pass, because hope was all that kept him from plummeting into despair. The carved angel might not be his finest work but she was the most important piece he had ever created, far more precious than elaborate staircases or rood screens, because she guarded the words of love Caro sent him. While Jack held these against his heart he would live, protected by his guardian angel and Caro's love. As long as he had the angel Jack knew he would be safe.

When on reaching into his pocket he had discovered the angel was missing Jack slipped into a tailspin of panic. He was so used to slipping his hand inside his rough jacket to feel the smooth curve of her wooden cheek, so accustomed to the solid bulk beneath the heel of his hand, that the absence was a shock akin to losing a part of himself. He wrestled his way out of his jacket, twisting and writing in a frantic attempt to free himself, before shaking it and checking over and over again in horrified disbelief.

The angel was gone, and with her Caro's words of love and hope.

With his heart a trapped bird fluttering beneath his ribcage, Jack buried his face in his hands. He was the closest to despair he had been since his arrival at the Front. There was no hope of setting off to find the angel now, for night had fallen, drawing to a close Christmas Day 1914 and the unofficial truce. Now there were no carols ringing out across the cratered earth, no cheery lights twinkling from makeshift Christmas trees, no festive greetings – only the forlorn moan of the winter wind and dark shadows of charred trees reaching out to the star-speckled heavens as though imploring peace to continue.

St Stephen's Day dawned grey and dismal, the elements as downcast as the men in the realisation that hostilities were to resume after that day of friendship. Already there was talk of a push forward and several patrols were preparing to venture out that night. Jack's hope was that he might be able to join one of them and search for the angel, but to his frustration he was ordered to give cover to a wiring party, keeping watch with his rifle trained on the enemy while they repaired the lines and strung up more of the cruelly barbed strands. It was a duty Jack always struggled with, for the standing still tested his busy mind, and his hands, forced to remain still, itched to carve and create. Today, with his mind filled with thoughts of retracing his footsteps, he knew that rather than straining his eyes for the enemy he would be scanning the frost-glazed world for a glimpse of hessian and wood.

It would be torture. If he was to be any use to his fellow soldiers he needed to find his angel but he had to do this alone, no matter what the personal risk, for he couldn't endanger his fellow soldiers. He could call it a scouting mission or say that he wanted to check out a place where a sniper could be stationed. Feeling determined now that he had a plan, Jack set off to put his case to Captain Rivers. The commanding officer was generally considered fair, and after carving the daisy for him Jack had a feeling that this man would understand more than any other exactly what the angel and Caro's letter meant to him.

Kit Rivers was seated at the table in the senior officers' dugout, working his way through a huge pile of paperwork. The stove was lit for coffee, but seeing Jack standing to attention in the doorway, he pushed the papers away.

"At ease, Tregenna," he said, rubbing his face wearily. "Unless it's more paperwork, in which case you're dismissed."

Jack smiled. Everyone knew the officers hated the endless paperwork. "I'm sorry to disturb you, sir. I wondered if I might have a word?"

Kit gestured at his mountain of memos and reports. "More of a welcome respite than a disturbance, Tregenna. I seem to spend far too much time writing reports about how many spare socks we have and the distinct lack of boots. I sometimes wonder if anyone even reads them? Maybe we should just send our old boots back instead as evidence? It might be more effective."

Jack glanced down at his own boots, which were falling apart. The cold weather had given them a respite from the mire, and even though the duckboard walkways were ice rinks rather than awash with sludge, they were usually sodden and his feet were always cold and damp. No matter how hard the men tried, it was impossible for them to dry out drenched socks and boots when life was subterranean, and it wasn't unusual for chunks of flesh to peel away with the wet wool. The need for new boots and socks was pressing, and became the focus of much conversation and resentment too, for how could they fight the enemy when they were in pain and limping? It was dangerous enough slipping when out on patrol, and a thousand times worse when you clomped and tripped along and alerted the enemy rather than moving with the stealth of a cat. Captain Rivers, appalled by the misery and hardship the men were enduring before they so much as even picked up a rifle, was working hard to make his superiors understand the importance of the issue, but so far he was having no luck and with bleeding feet the men trudged on in disintegrating boots.

Jack wanted to nod and say that they would soon be marching barefoot if the Army didn't organise more boots, but he knew it wasn't his place to do so. Caro's new, more egalitarian, world had yet to materialise. "Sir," was all he said.

Kit pressed the heels of his hands against his eyes and yawned widely. "Sorry. I was on periscope duty until the small hours," he said, rising from the table and stretching out his cramped limbs. "Captain Elmhurst had a notion the enemy might take advantage of yesterday's truce now they have a better idea of our position. I told him it was Christmas and peace on earth and all that but, as he's a lawyer, cynicism flows through his veins."

"The Germans must fear exactly the same thing. They're not so different to us," Jack pointed out, thinking of again of Heinrich and unable to stop himself. "We all saw that yesterday, sir."

Kit looked at him thoughtfully. "Indeed, Tregenna, although I can't imagine that observation is something the generals will want repeated. Truces are perhaps not conducive to effective warfare. Man cannot fight unless he sees the enemy as other to himself."

His summer-sky eyes met Jack's and the expression they held was bleak. Neither man said any more on the matter, but

Jack understood there would be no more truces and no more occasions to lay down weapons and talk. His heart sank, and the gloomy day above them seemed to become even greyer as the shine of Christmas friendship between foes was extinguished. There would be no end to the war this Christmas, Jack realised, only more offensives and more death. Would he ever leave this place and see Caro again? Feel the Cornish sea mist against his face and inhale the salt-sprinkled air? He *had* to find his angel, Jack realised with rising dread, for he needed her to keep him safe more now than ever before. It seemed that the Christmas truce had made the situation even more precarious.

"Sir," he said again, and helplessness dulled his voice. "Yes, sir."

"But you don't want to listen to me philosophising," said Kit Rivers wearily. "What was it you wanted, Lieutenant?"

Jack sought to articulate what he felt without sounding unhinged. When spoken aloud to an officer, he feared that his conviction of the lost angel's importance would seem little more than a superstition. He knew that leaving the cover of the trench in order to attempt a recovery would be a foolish and unnecessary risk. The captain might think him mad, or fear that he was suffering the effects of shelling. Some men fell to the ground insensible with terror, so why should others not have delusions about carved angels?

"Tregenna?"

Kit was waiting for him to speak, and for a moment Jack considered inventing an excuse requiring him to venture outside the cover of the trench, some elaborate tale about needing to check hiding places for a sniper's position, perhaps. Or maybe he would funk telling the truth entirely and make an unauthorised foray beyond the wire. Nobody would be any the wiser. He didn't need to mention the angel at all.

Yet there was something about the captain's quiet authority which inspired confidence. He couldn't lie to Kit, Jack realised. He didn't want to deceive a commanding officer who was fair and brave. In spite of his reservations the words poured out in a torrent of truth, and the commanding officer listened carefully until Jack had talked himself to a standstill.

Then Kit exhaled and shook his head regretfully. "I can't authorise a patrol so you can search for your angel, Tregenna. It would be putting men at unnecessary risk."

"I understand, sir," said Jack. Disappointment hit him in the guts, a sucker punch of misery. "It sounds quite mad, I know that. Superstitious even."

"It's not for me to judge. Lord knows a man needs something out here to hold onto and keep the faith of returning."

"Can I go alone?" Jack suggested, clinging to hope that the understanding Kit might relent.

But his hopes were soon dashed for the captain was appalled by the suggestion. "Absolutely not! I can't allow you to risk yourself for the sake of recovering a talisman. You could inadvertently risk all of us. I won't allow it, Tregenna, and that's an order."

"What if I went by myself? At my own risk?"

"It's too dangerous. I totally forbid you from making an unofficial venture beyond the wire. If you do, I will personally have you court-martialled. Do I make myself clear, Lieutenant Tregenna? Do I?"

Jack's heart tumbled into his disintegrating boots. He could not blatantly disobey an officer he both liked and respected, not even to find his lost angel. He couldn't speak.

Kit Rivers was troubled by Jack's lack of reply. "Tregenna.

That's an order. Do you understand? I will not countenance an excursion beyond the wire."

"Yes, sir," Jack said bleakly. "I understand."

"Good," said Kit. "I'm glad to hear it. I don't want to hear any more on the matter. Dismissed."

"Sir."

Jack stood to attention and saluted. He was close to despair, for there was no hope of finding the angel now. She was lost to him, and so was the certainty he would return to Caro. Yet again he had the strongest premonition that he would never see her again.

"Tregenna," Kit said softly as he was leaving.

Jack turned back. "Sir?"

"You don't need an angel, Jack." Kit lay a hand on his chest just over his heart, and smiled at him, a small sad smile that spoke of heartache and of understanding. "It's all in here. That's where you'll find comfort, and that's what'll bring you home. It's all the talisman you need."

The captain was right, Jack reflected as he returned to his quarters. Love would bring him home. The angel bore Caro's likeness, but although the angel was lost their love for one another never would be. Jack was determined that he would live to carve a hundred more angels. He *would* become a sculptor and a success. He *would* marry Caro, and together they would build the family, the home and the beautiful life they dreamed of. The war would not keep them apart. Wherever the lost angel might be, Jack hoped that any man who might have scooped her up from the torn earth would be comforted. British or German, she would watch over him from now on.

Her work for him, Jack, was done.

Heartened, he turned for his dugout at the very moment

the shelling began. It ripped through the stillness and seemed to be everywhere all at once, a roar of death amid cries of wounded men. The sky was flickering and dancing with light all the way north, and the earth bucked beneath Jack's feet. Clods of earth hit him like pummelling fists and his nostrils were filled with dirt and the tang of smoke. Coughing and choking, he dropped to his hands and knees and fought to breathe through the smoke and showers of earth. His heart was beating hard and he was shaking with shock at this direct attack on their lines.

So much for peace on earth. The enemy had aimed straight at them. Was Heinrich even now watching through field glasses and ordering his men to fire again? Jack hoped not, but this was a world turned upside down, and as the earth heaved once again he knew this analogy was also a literal observation.

"The trench is hit!" he heard somebody call. "Take cover in the back one. Go!"

Booted feet scrabbled and slipped on iced duckboards. Cries of fear and anger plugged Jack's ears, and as earth rained down on him again he coughed and spluttered. The ground lurched once again, a living creature trying to vomit shells, and Jack's hands slithered on the ice. Try as he might, he could not get to his feet to run for cover. In the mayhem and smoke and noise it was impossible to tell where he should go, he realised, even if he was able to stand. It was all he could do to draw air into his lungs. He screwed his eyes up and began to crawl in the direction he seemed to recall was correct, keeping his head below the smoke. Caro's love would keep him safe. He had to hold onto that. Their story didn't end here in alien soil and far away from the beaches and soft rains of Cornwall. It couldn't ...

There was another blast and a flash of light so beautifully bright he gasped with amazement. Then more earth was hurled at him and he was slammed into the mire, his nose and mouth filling with muddy water as his breath was snatched away. There was a white-hot pain in his forehead and a strange buzzing in his ears and then all was silent and Jack wanted nothing more than to sleep. He was so very tired, he thought wearily, and to close his eyes would be such bliss. A few moments of rest wouldn't hurt ...

"Jack! Jack!"

To his amazement and delight, Caro was just ahead of him in the swirl of smoke and dirt, with her hand outstretched and her gentle voice calling him forwards. She was just a kiss away, close enough to almost touch! If he clawed his way through the mire and the darkness, inch by painful inch, he would surely reach her, and this knowledge filled Jack with such joy that he couldn't help laughing. As the shells rained down and the earth shuddered Jack thought he had never been so glad to be here, for look – there was Caro! Even the sticky warmth of blood dripping into his eyes and the savage pain in his head couldn't dim his happiness, for what did such things matter now that Caro was here? Jack's heart was overflowing with happiness.

"Caro," he whispered as the darkness closed around him. "My Caro."

When they dug him out nearly three days later, Jack Tregenna, bloodied and unmoving, was still smiling.

10

The Present
Cornwall
Ellen

THE VILLAGE CHURCH couldn't have changed very much since Caroline Sweethouse had sat in her pew to pray for Jack's safe return. Now, as in Caro and Jack's day, St Julietta's was filled with a deep eiderdown of peace which sank into the soul, and the hushed air was rich with the prayers of centuries. Fingers of sunlight stroked worn flagstones, dipped in places from the generations of prayerful feet passing to the altar rail, and the wintry sunshine poured in through the windows and rippled across the walls and floor. Ellen loved it straight away.

A small Christmas tree by the door sparkled with colourful fairy lights, a large crib with gaudy nativity figures was in prime position by the lectern, and swathes of holly and ivy tied with scarlet bows adorned the windowsills and twisted up the stone arches, but apart from these festive splashes of brightness the whitewashed church was a simple affair. It was a place to worship rather than a memorial of some past benefactor's wealth and earthly glory, and Ellen thought she would choose the word 'restful' to describe the place. She wasn't surprised that Caro had found solace here, for whether or not you believed in God this holy place vibrated with an energy that came from a thousand years or more of prayer. The veil between past and present felt thin here – so thin it seemed to her only moments ago that Jack and Caro had worshipped. Perhaps to a building this old and holy a hundred years was only minutes in the eternal scheme of things?

The simplicity of St. Julietta's might have been due to Reformation zeal, as Bev explained, and intended to squash any lurking Catholic sympathies, but it served as the perfect foil to the beautiful wooden screen which divided the chancel from the nave. As Bev described the purpose of the screen and pointed out all its unique features, Ellen stared up at it in wonder. The talent of the craftsman who'd created this was without question, and the piece was far more than ecclesiastical furniture – it was art.

"Arts and Crafts actually," said Bev, when Ellen made this point. "Medieval art is apparently the inspiration for that movement. "I think that's why John – or Jack – Tregenna's early work is so valuable. He used wood rather than stone, and it has medieval influences too, like that drunken little gargoyle peeking out at the top. He's even got a tankard!"

"It's stunning," Anna said. "Look at the leaves on that vine. They have veins!"

The work was intricate: every hair on the coats of the shy forest creatures peering through the greenery bristled, feathers fluttered on the outstretched wings of birds, and the wood itself seemed to glow with vibrant life. The lacework of delicate tracery linking the entire piece was gossamer fragile as a spider's web, and the Christ figure hung at the apex so torn and agonised that Ellen had to look away from his suffering.

Yet as breathtaking as all the details were, it was not these which caused Ellen to gasp, but rather the angels gracing the very top of the screen and dancing in the heavens with saints and chubby cherubim. The more closely she looked, the more of them she saw peeking through the greenery or with woodland creatures, and she was moved to see how each angel bore the beautiful face of her own angel.

The face which belonged to Caro Sweethouse, Jack's great love.

"Is your angel the same as those?" asked Anna pointing at the top of the screen.

"Yes," said Ellen. She didn't even need to look at her angel to know that she was identical. The sweet smile, the curve of the cheek, the perfect lips, the cascade of carved curls – all these were mirror images of the battered decoration found in Granny Clara's cupboard. There was no doubt that Jack Tregenna was the man who had carved this rood. She withdrew the angel from her pocket and held her up so they could see the similarity.

"Oh my! There's no mistaking that. You really do have an original Tregenna piece!" said Bev.

"So Jack and John Tregenna *were* the same person," Anna concluded. "He survived the war and became a famous sculptor."

"He must have done," said Ellen. She felt close to tears at this good news. Was it crazy to be this relieved that a man who must have been dead for decades had survived the war?

"He came home, married Caro, became successful and lived happily ever after."

"They probably married here," said Bev. "I can check the register later, if you like."

"I'd love that," said Ellen. How she hoped Caro had drifted up the aisle in lace and silk to join Jack at the altar rail.

Anna shot her a smug look. "See? Romances do have happy endings, Ellen. Not everything ends in doom and gloom."

Ellen laughed. "There's hope for me yet, you mean?"

"Your granny thought so."

"Granny Clara was a hopeless romantic."

"No such thing; there's always hope," Bev told her. "Look at your Jack Tregenna. He came back from the war against all the odds and became more successful than he probably ever imagined when he was living in the village making furniture. Your little angel will be worth a fortune to a gallery or a private collector."

"I couldn't sell her!" Ellen was horrified. How could she part with Granny Clara's angel? She wasn't a commodity.

Besides, she wasn't really Ellen's, was she?

She belonged to Caroline Sweethouse or rather she belonged to Jack and Caro's descendants.

"I understand," Bev said. She pointed to the rood screen. "Some things are beyond a monetary price, aren't they?"

Ellen nodded. "Anyway, she's not mine to sell. This angel was made for Caroline Sweethouse and I have no idea how my grandfather came by it, but I do know it doesn't belong to me. It belongs to Jack and Caro's family, and I'm going to give it back to them."

Although the church was cold – so cold that her own

breath was rising in little clouds and Anna had her hands wedged into her armpits to keep them from turning blue – Ellen felt a warm glow, and a shard of sunlight filtered down to pool at her feet. Somebody approved of her decision, she was sure of it.

"You're nuts, Elly. I may need to stage an intervention," groaned Anna. "It must be worth a bomb – right, Reverend?"

The vicar laughed. "Ah, the call of Mammon! You'd need to talk to an expert in such things, but yes, I imagine the angel will be of great interest to the art world as it's such an early one and it has a story too. People love a tragic story – look at the Kit Rivers film."

"But Jack and Caro must have married if he came home," said Ellen. "Their story is a happy one."

"True, but this angel is unusual and would be rare because it must have been created before John Tregenna lost his sight. The bulk of his work was created post war."

Ellen stared at her. The flagstones surged beneath her feet and she steadied herself by holding onto a pew.

"What do you mean, 'lost his sight'?" she whispered.

"Oh, didn't I mention it? John Tregenna was blind," said Bev airily and totally unaware that she was dropping a bombshell. "He lost his sight during the war. Makes his achievements even more remarkable, wouldn't you say? To not be able to see yet still create beautiful works of art?"

Ellen was shocked. The Jack of Caro's letter, the strong young man who strode across the cliffs and gazed at the cloud-hugged horizon, had spent the rest of his life unable to see the face of the woman he loved? The face that was bequeathed to all the angels up on the rood screen and her lost angel was denied to him? It was so unbearably sad, and she had to swallow hard. Although Jack and Caro were long gone, sliding from memory and into history, to her they were still eighteen and vibrant with life and dreams and confidence in the future. Knowing what lay ahead for the young couple was heart-breaking.

"What happened to him?"

"Explosions or shelling, I imagine. I suppose I ought to find out really, because it's the kind of thing visitors like to know," confessed Bev. She glanced at her watch and grimaced. "Lord! I'm running late again. The nativity committee will have my guts for garters. I have to scoot, I'm afraid, but feel free to stay and look around. There are some very interesting brasses too."

But Ellen wasn't interested in brasses. "You mentioned that the Tregenna family still live here?"

"That's right. There's an elderly lady, Cécile, and her son. They've put the house on the market, actually, so you're just in time because that place will sell in seconds. I bet they'd be thrilled to see the letter and the angel."

But Ellen wasn't so sure. After all, nobody knew quite how her great-grandfather had come by Jack Tregenna's lost angel. What if the answer was one she would rather not know? The landscape of history was dotted with treacherous quicksands, and perhaps some secrets were best left slumbering in the past. The Tregenna family might not welcome a direct descendant of Heinrich Schneider.

Ellen was about to ask Bev for some more details about the Tregenna family but a volley of barks from the porch sent the vicar sprinting out there. By the time Adam and Eve had been pulled apart and ticked off, the vicar was running really late for the nativity play rehearsal. Christmas was her busiest time, she explained breathlessly while attempting to untangle the dogs' leads, and everyone wanted the church and the vicar all of a sudden. Deciding it wasn't fair to delay Bev any further when she'd already given up so much of her time, Ellen supposed she would have to put on her big girl pants and visit Sea Angel. The First World War was a very long time ago. Surely nobody held any animosity now to the descendants of German soldiers?

She guessed there was only one way to find out.

11

1915

Bristol

Caro

At first all, she felt was relief. Jack was alive. He was leaving the dangers of the Front and he would return to Cornwall and to her. What else mattered except that he was safe? It could have been so much worse, everyone said so. He could have been dead.

Caro knew she was fortunate. So many other young women were dressed in mourning these days, engagement rings loose on their fingers and their eyes shadowed with sadness, while others were tortured daily by fear that the telegram boy would lean his bike against their garden gate, rap on the door and deliver the news that everyone dreaded. It was hard to navigate the motions of ordinary life when fear cast its shadowy cloak over every moment.

Before her turn had come she had been braced for bad

news. Whenever she sat at the desk in the morning room to discuss menus with the housekeeper, Caro's attention strayed from the merits of tongue over ham and whisked her over the miles to Jack. It was impossible to think of anything else. Her own studies were dreadfully neglected, and even reading, always her solace, became impossible, for her concentration was torn to ribbons and she found herself reading the same sentences over and over again without absorbing their meaning. Jack was all she could think about and whenever a surge of terror threatened to sweep her off her feet, she focused every ounce of concentration she possessed on willing him back to her once more.

It was as though from the moment the train pulled away from Rosecraddick Halt taking Jack away from her and to war, a pane of glass had slipped between her and the rest of the world. As if her heart had been pierced by the sliver of ice from the Snow Queen, Caro's feelings were frozen and she found herself sleepwalking through the days. There was no joy to be found in the pink and rose gold sunsets, no laughter bubbled up from her soul when Bramble fetched a ball. The world with all its beauty was muffled and muted. Until she held Jack Tregenna in her arms once more, Caro Sweethouse would only be half-alive.

So how was it possible that for others life continued to run in its familiar and well-worn tracks? How could petty concerns such as the infestation of slugs in the vegetable garden, or her papa's annoyance when he misplaced a book, be deemed important when men were dying in their thousands and a new widow was made with each tick of the Rectory's grandfather clock? Was this evidence of the resilience of the human spirit in the face of unimaginable horrors? Or proof that others around her lacked imagination?

Caro couldn't decide. She only knew that for her, reading daily about the ugliness of this war steeped her in an agony of fear. It felt almost insulting that in Penmarloe the tides still turned, seagulls rather than aeroplanes swooped through the cloudless sky, and a blissfully unaware Bramble chased birds through a garden long unmown and gone rogue. Surely the whole world should have paused until Jack and all the other young men came home? Or was the continued importance of minutiae the only way that it was possible to place one foot in front of the other to keep on the path without teetering into the ravines which lay either side?

Her own plunge into the abyss arrived one bleak morning towards the end of December, when the bitter weather had pared the world to little more than shards of ice and pimpled plough, and even the grey sea seemed to shiver. Caro had been in the drawing room attempting to coax the fire into life with damp kindling and newspaper curls when the squeak of the garden gate made her glance up. A cold clutch of dread squeezed her heart when she saw Jack's mother straightening her hat and walking along the path. Maud Tregenna wouldn't usually dream of calling at the front door of the Rectory, even though it was home to her future daughter-in-law, unless there was a very important reason.

A reason she would have to share in person ...

Feeling as though she was in a dream, Caro sent Betty away and answered the door herself. In a peculiar way she was relieved that this most dreaded moment had arrived. It had haunted her every waking and sleeping moment for so long that to be faced with it became a release from the agony of living in the suspended animation of terror. When she'd allowed herself to imagine this moment she had always pictured herself falling down in a faint or crumpling to the floor as her legs gave way and a tempest of tears swept through her – yet now the moment had arrived she was too numb to react at all.

Opening the door, she studied Maud Tregenna closely for evidence of grief.

"Is it Jack?" she blurted, unable to stop herself. "Is he … is he …?" She couldn't say the words. They lodged in her throat threatening to choke her. To speak them aloud would make the unthinkable real.

Maud Tregenna took Caro's hands in hers and clasped them tightly. Her green eyes, so heart-breakingly familiar, gazed into Caro's and swam with tears. "My dear, you must be very brave. Jack's been wounded."

Caro stared at her. The tiled floor seemed to surge beneath her feet. "Wounded? He's alive?"

Maud nodded. Her chin was wobbling and she swallowed before speaking. "He is, but only just. He's badly injured, Caro."

Caro didn't hear another word; the relief of her Jack being alive was so overwhelming that she felt as though she'd downed an entire bottle of her Papa's best Amontillado. Maud's mouth was opening and closing but there was no sound and the hallway carouselled in a whirl of tiles and cornicing and gleaming banisters. Time contracted, for now her father was there, holding her up and guiding her into the drawing room. Only once Caro was seated and holding a cup of sweet tea in shaking hands did the buzzing in her ears cease and the room stop spinning.

Jack was alive. He was wounded and in hospital, but he was alive. He would come home now. What did injuries matter? She would nurse him back to health and they would be together. She would make soups and nourishing food to coax back his appetite, and they would take short walks together in the garden. The fresh salty air would put colour back in his cheeks, and with her love and care Jack would soon be strong once more. Oh! She couldn't wait to see him again and to see his dear face. Injuries were as nothing in the face of losing him forever.

While she sipped her tea, Caro and her father listened to Maud explain how shelling had taken place along the front line with Jack's trench receiving a direct hit. He was lucky to be alive, Maud said, as she mopped her eyes with the handkerchief Reverend Sweethouse had gallantly offered her, for the young man Jack had been standing beside had been killed outright. Everyone agreed it could have been so much worse. Jack Tregenna had an angel watching over him, that was for sure.

Maud finished her tea and set the cup down in the saucer with a clatter. She had talked herself to a standstill yet somehow told them nothing. All Caro had gleaned was that Jack was injured and in a field hospital. As soon as he was deemed well enough to be moved he would be transferred to a convalescent hospital back in England. He would never return to the Front. Jack's war was over.

It seemed like a miracle to Caro.

The Reverend Sweethouse remained silent while Jack's mother spoke, but his expression remained grave even in the face of what sounded like good news. He poured himself a second cup of tea, dropping in a lump of sugar with silver tongs and stirring it thoughtfully.

"What exactly are his injuries?" he asked eventually.

"I don't really know," Maud admitted. "The telegram only says he's wounded and grievously ill. I expect I'll learn more in due course. I was just so relieved the news wasn't what I'd feared, for the telegram looked just like the one Jessie Trehunnist received when she lost her Sam. I thought the worst."

The Reverend nodded, and the conversation turned to how Caro would write to Jack and the possibility of her travelling out to France to visit him at the field hospital. The Rector thought he might call at Rosecraddick Manor and ask if Colonel Rivers might be able to help them find out more, since Jack was in his old regiment. Maybe his son Kit would be able to help her reach Jack's side? Caro had only met Kit a handful of times but he struck her as a kind young man and she was suddenly filled with optimism. All would be well.

But once Maud Tregenna had departed, the Reverend turned to Caro and his face was troubled. "My dear, you must prepare yourself for the worst."

Caro's hands, hidden in the folds of her skirts, clenched. Bramble, dozing at her feet, sensed the tension and sat up with a sharp bark.

"Jack won't die, Papa. He'll come home to me just as he promised," she said.

Her father tugged at his beard and said nothing.

"He will," Caro insisted.

"Some injuries are worse than death," said Reverend Sweethouse gently. "You surely understand what I am saying, my dear?"

"What does it matter to me if he's lost limbs if Jack is still alive? Do you really think I'm so shallow, Papa?" Caro flared.

"I'm not thinking about limbs, my dear, although those injuries bring their own issues. I'm concerned about injuries that may change everything for you both and create terrible hardship in the years ahead. Disfigurement is a possibility, as are the type of injuries that might prevent him from fathering children. They also say some men are suffering from psychiatric disorders and violent episodes. Will you be able to manage these things, Caroline? And what if he cannot work to keep you and take care of you? What then?"

Caro raised her chin.

"Then we'll face those things together, Papa, whatever they may be. 'Love is not love which alters when it alteration finds', remember?"

He raised his eyebrows. "That's easy for poets to say, but I fear a little harder in practice. I shall pray for Jack and for you too, my dear. I suppose we shall find out presently how bad things are, and then we'll be able to make some decisions about whether or not this marriage goes ahead. You are, as you are well aware, not yet of age."

She stared at him in disbelief. "Are you saying you'll withdraw your blessing if Jack is badly hurt?"

"As your father, it is my responsibility to have a care for your future," he replied, rising to his feet and thus ending the conversation. "Since your dear mama is no longer with us, it is one I take most seriously since it is all mine."

Caro bit back the sharp retort which flew to her lips. She knew her father only had her best interests at heart, for each day the newspapers were full of descriptions of the horrific injuries sustained by men fighting on the Front. She refused to be downcast, for Jack was saved from the fighting and at some point he would be coming home where she would nurse him back to health and care for him. All would be well. If he had lost a leg, or even both, it wouldn't affect his ability to create sculpture, and even if he had lost an arm she felt certain he would adapt. The man she loved was strong and resourceful. Jack would never admit defeat and he would find a way to make a life for them and to create the works of art which burned in his soul and called to be set free into marble. All would be well. Really, Jack was one of the lucky ones.

A day later, Maud passed on more news she had received; although Jack had taken a nasty wound to his shoulder, she said, the doctors were confident that he would make a full physical recovery – so Caro's father's worst fears of lost limbs and disfigurement had not been realised – but Jack's eyes, caught in the full force of the blast and splintered with shrapnel, were badly damaged. They were unlikely to heal, and Jack would never see the sunsets and the seascapes that had so lifted his heart.

Caro knew he would never again gaze down with love into her eyes. He would never see their children.

Jack Tregenna, artist, sculptor and keeper of her heart, was blind.

She wept long and hard when she learned this, and she wept even harder on reading the letter Jack had written to her from France, in a spidery hand that veered wildly down the page and bore little resemblance to his old and elegant hand. He loved her, he said, and thought of her every day. He missed her more than he could ever say, but he was afraid of what the future held for them now and although he did not say it, she knew he feared that she would no longer love or want him. He was adamant she shouldn't travel to France and visit him, and insisted that she wait until he was ready.

I am not as I was, he wrote, *for none of us who are in this place are the men we used to be. When I have made my peace with that then you can decide whether you still wish to see me. Please know that I love you still and that although I cannot see you with my eyes, every moment of the day my heart sees you still.*

In the end Reverend Sweethouse did not need to visit

Colonel Rivers and Caro didn't need to find a way of travelling to France for, as hoped, Jack was swiftly transferred to a hospital in Calais, then on to a convalescent home, in Bristol.

Although everything in Caro longed to fly to Jack's bedside she understood he needed time alone. He had to concentrate on regaining his own strength without having to shoulder her grief too, and because she loved him so much she fought her yearning to see him, no matter how much it pained her not to be able to hold him close to comfort him and tell him that nothing, *nothing,* would ever change her love for him. Instead she had to be patient, and she spent more and more time sitting in St Julietta's where she gazed up at the angels which bore her own face and implored them to heal Jack's heart as well as his body and eyes.

Time clomped past as though shod in lead boots as Caro waited for Jack to ask her to visit him. Although Jack wrote that according to the doctors his physical injuries were mending well, Caro knew the deeper and invisible injuries were far from healed. There was no point in attempting to argue with her fiancé or talk him around; the man she loved so dearly had always been set on making his own way in the world and proving he was worthy of her. Losing his sight would only exacerbate such traits and, although she admired his pride and his determination, Caro's darkest fear was that Jack might never reconcile himself with this cruel twist of Fate and choose to set her free.

And that would break her heart.

Finally a letter arrived inviting her to visit the hospital in Bristol where Jack was convalescing. The invite came in the shape of a formal epistle, in a tone unlike anything Jack had written previously. Each line crackled with tension as though the ink had absorbed all his fears, and every word seemed to echo with a distance borne from his witnessing the horrors which only those at the Front could comprehend. If Caro would like to visit, Jack wrote politely, she was most welcome to come the following week. Visiting hours were in the afternoon and on Wednesdays there was high tea available with fruit cake and scones and which was generally agreed to be excellent.

Caro couldn't care less about afternoon tea – her appetite had dwindled away to almost nothing lately – but she did care about Jack, and her spirits rose to know she would see him after so long. She wrote back immediately accepting his invitation for the very next Wednesday, and saying she could hardly wait for the cake and scones. As always she reminded Jack how much she loved him and how terribly she had missed him, hoping that he would hold these words close and open his heart to her again. She knew she would never stop loving him, and could only pray he wouldn't choose to turn away.

When the day of the visit arrived and the dogcart dropped her at Rosecraddick Halt, Caro felt sick with excitement and dread. She boarded the train and opened her book, hoping for a distraction from her nerves, but the words kept blurring and dancing until she had to abandon reading altogether. Instead, she gazed out of the window and as the landscape unfolded the journey seemed like a dream. As the grey water and red cliffs of Dawlish gave way to the lush fields of the Exe valley then the waterlogged Somerset levels, Caro had felt as though she was in a liminal zone between the old life with Jack and the new and unknown one which lay ahead.

The convalescent facility was in Clifton and rather than the austere building she had expected – like the sanatorium in Penhayes where those unlucky enough to suffer from consumption were sent to recover in blasts of bracing sea air and watery sunshine – it was set in a commandeered private house overlooking the graceful sweep of the suspension bridge and sparkling waters of the Avon flowing beneath. The owners' luxurious furnishings and fittings had been removed and the papered walls bore bright squares where paintings had once hung, but even so Caro felt more as though she was about to take tea with a grand dowager than visit her injured fiancé. Only glimpses of men with missing limbs taking the air on the elegant terrace – some leaning heavily on the arms of nurses and others nimble on crutches – and muffled groans from behind closed doors hinted at the new nature of the place.

Following a nurse up the sweeping staircase, Caro raised her face to the light which streamed through the long window above the return. The naked limbs of trees shivered against a bright winter sky, shockingly cloudless and blue against the rooftops of Bristol which tumbled away below, sparkling in the frost and as magical as a storybook scene. The juxtaposition of such dreadful injuries and the beauty of the wintry city added to the sense of unreality that had saturated her every moment since Jack had enlisted.

Very soon she would see him again. Would he still love her? Want to hold her and kiss her? Or would the time apart and the avalanche of experiences they could never share drive a wedge between them? Could they move onwards from this? Caro felt certain that they could, for she loved Jack with all her heart and would do whatever it took to help him fashion a new life for himself. She only prayed he would feel the same and that he wouldn't choose to turn away from her through some misguided sense of setting her free. A life without him held no liberty for Caro, but would rather be a prison of loss and loneliness. She was blessed he was alive, she thought with a flutter of the gratitude, for many wives, mothers and sweethearts were not as fortunate.

Feeling even more nervous than she had expected, Caro followed the nurse along the darkened corridor that led away from the top of the ornate staircase. Once it had been flooded with light from the elegant sashes, but today each window was blinded by heavy drapes which sealed away the sunshine and plunged the place into gloom.

"It's better for the patients," explained the nurse when Caro asked why this might be the case. "Lots of them suffer with their nerves, and being agitated is the worst thing for them. Darkness soothes the patients. It's healing."

Caro couldn't help wondering if the sombre atmosphere might have the opposite effect. Surely the young men who had suffered so greatly would benefit from light and the life it brought? To her way of thinking the hope of spring would help greatly to counter the despair they must have suffered while fighting in the trenches and seeing horrors she couldn't even begin, or indeed want, to imagine. The darkness closed around her like a fist, and she fought the urge to rip the curtains open.

"This is his room." The nurse opened a door into a large and gloomy room. A floor-to-ceiling window was shrouded in drapes, a deep maroon waterfall beneath a pelmet festooned with ornate gilt ropes, and a bed was set beneath, parallel to the sill. A young man lay on the creased counterpane, propped up on pillows with his head turned away from the door and towards where the light would be if it was allowed into the room, and he started when the door creaked open. Although his eyes were swathed in white bandages and his body was far thinner than Caro recalled, she would have known the sweet smile anywhere. She'd dreamed of seeing it for so long. She was hardly able to believe she was finally close enough to touch him and hold him tightly.

Jack. Her beloved Jack.

"There's a bell if you need anything," said the nurse when Caro didn't move.

"Thank you."

To Caro's relief her voice was even, though she was quaking inside. The daisies trembled in her hands and she laid them on the table before reaching into her pocket and closing her fingers around the carved angel. The familiar warmth of the smooth wood beneath her fingertips steadied her heartbeat. This was an anchor to hold her fast in this churning sea of nerves, uncertainty and excitement. It was a link between their past and the present.

The door clicked shut behind the nurse and at last they were alone. Jack turned his head and he smiled at her, a wan smile of such uncertainty that if her heart hadn't already been breaking to see him so dreadfully wounded it would have surely shattered into a thousand pieces to glimpse this fear of rejection.

"Caro," he whispered. "My Caro."

"Oh Jack."

His name came as a sob both of happiness and of distress, for how could it be that those deep green eyes would never look at her again? To watch his bandaged face turn towards the sound of her voice broke her heart. It was so cruel.

Overcome with emotion, all her powers of speech fled. She was rooted to the spot.

"Are you really here?" Jack asked. "Truly, Caro? You're here."

"Yes," she whispered, still standing by the door. "I'm here. I would have been here before if you'd have let me."

"It wasn't pretty, Caro. I was nothing more than bandages for a time and I didn't want to put you through it. You didn't need to see what I was. What I had become."

"That wasn't your choice to make!" Her savage anger took her by surprise. She had imagined this reconciliation so many times, playing scenarios through her mind's eye, and she had always envisaged herself falling into Jack's arms. She had never once dreamed all the months of missing him and living in fear, followed by the shock of his injury and then being kept from Jack's side at his own instigation, would boil up inside her and erupt in a volcano of hurt rage.

"What about what *I* wanted, Jack?" she cried. "What about me needing you? Did you ever think about that? Do you think so little of me that you think it would change how I feel about you?"

He swallowed. "I was scared."

"So was I!" Caro shot back, suddenly enraged. "I was terrified and I needed you, Jack. How could you have kept me away? How could you have been so cruel?"

"Because of this!" He ripped off his bandages and hurled them to the floor. "Look at me! Can you live with this? Can you?"

Caro's anger evaporated in an instant. Before she had been escorted to his room the nurse had warned her that he was badly hurt, but nothing had prepared her for the reality. She forced herself not to look away from the puckered scarlet flesh and sightless eyes. She would not recoil from the ravaged face of the man she loved. Not even so much as a gasp left her lips. If Jack had to bear this then she certainly could.

And he was alive. What mattered more than that?

"Oh Jack," she said softly. "What you don't understand is that I can't live *without* it."

But Jack shook his head.

"No, Caro. How can you bring yourself to love me like this? I wouldn't blame you if you felt you can't. I would never expect you to keep to our engagement now everything has changed. Now I'm like this." He shook his head. "I release you from any promises. You're free to go."

She stared at him, shocked. "Go? What do you mean?"

"Walk away. I want you to have a full and happy life. Don't shackle yourself to me, Caro. You deserve more. You deserve the world." His voice cracked. "I want you to have it. You shouldn't have to see me like this. I never wanted this for you."

Jack's heartbreak was palpable and suddenly Caro understood why he had kept her away for all these months – he'd needed time to gather the strength to tell her to walk away. He'd been only thinking of her and protecting her, and she ached to think just how much he had suffered.

"*You* are my world," she said simply. "Nothing could change the way I feel about you. Nothing at all. I love you, Jack. *You.* Not your eyes or your talent or your face. *You.*"

Jack Tregenna was more than eyes or his vision. Those things had been cruelly snatched away, but the essence of him, the purity of heart and the love distilled, made him the man she loved and these had not changed. He was her beloved Jack, and she would love him until she took her final breath.

"Don't send me away," she said, and her voice cracked. "Please, Jack. Don't do that to us. Please."

"You could still love me?" He pointed to his poor burned face and the unseeing eyes. "You could love me like *this*?"

Love sluiced through Caro and she thought she might drown in the floodtide of emotion. In answer to his agonised question she ran to his side, taking his hand and pressing it against her lips over and over again as she told him that she loved him more than ever. Then she kissed his forehead, the puckered red skin of his burned eyelids and finally his beautiful mouth. Jack's lips trembled beneath hers, and he inhaled sharply as though unable to believe she was there holding him and kissing him and telling him over and over again how much she loved him, had missed him and would always want to be with him. Then, like a man finally reaching the end of a long journey, he groaned and was kissing her back, whispering the words she had longed to hear for so long.

"Oh Caro, my own darling Caro. I love you so much. Not a minute has passed when I haven't longed for you. I'll always love you. Always."

"I'll always love you too," Caro choked. "Never doubt that. Always and forever. No matter what."

"I know," he said. "I think I always did, but it was hard to hold onto that when ..."

"Don't," she begged, knowing he was thinking of how he must appear to her. "That's the least of who we are. You're here, Jack. We have a future, and it's going to be wonderful."

He cupped her cheek with his hand. "I can still see you. I've never stopped seeing you."

"You always saw me," Caro reminded him. "The real me, I mean, not the Rector's daughter. The girl who reads and argues and runs along the beach and who dreams of so much more. You saw her, Jack."

"You saw me too."

"I certainly did. I thought you were some kind of sea god standing half-naked on the beach!" she recalled, laughing. "I thought I'd swoon. You probably wondered why I couldn't speak!"

Jack laughed too. "I was struck dumb by you! I thought it was an angel on the path. But I didn't mean that. I meant that you saw what I could be. Not the carpenter's lad. You saw the angel in the marble."

"I see it still," she said quietly. "And I know you will carve until you set it free."

Slipping from his embrace, she withdrew the wooden angel from her coat pocket and, placing it into his hands, closed his fingers around it.

"The angel!" Jack exclaimed.

"The first of many, remember? You promised many, many more and I'm going to hold you to that promise, Jack Tregenna. While you were away I carried her everywhere. She helped me feel closer to you."

Jack pressed the carving to his lips.

"I carried one too. She was a rough creature made from odds and ends, and not my finest work, but I treasured her. I kept your first letter tucked inside her secret place to keep you close. I hoped to bring her home so you could have her for Christmas, as I'd promised I would – but I lost her. I knew then that my luck was running out. In that place, how could it not?"

His sightless eyes were staring into the corner of the room and Caro understood he was seeing another place, one where mud and shells and horror lay in wait for the fresh-faced boys who had set off there with such high hopes. She said nothing, but her heart hurt to think of all he had suffered.

"I wanted to search for her but it was impossible," Jack

continued, tugging himself back into the present. "She was lost in No Man's Land. I think I must have dropped her on Christmas Day during the truce."

Caro had heard the stories. "That really happened?"

"Oh yes, it happened all right. I spoke with one of their officers for a while, a nice man who was a schoolteacher, and I played football with our boys and theirs. The angel must have fallen out of my pocket. I was devastated, Caro. It felt like losing you."

She rested her hand on his shoulder. "You'll never lose me."

"But I lost your angel. I promised you one every Christmas for the rest of my life, didn't I? Losing her meant breaking my promise to you, and that broke my heart. That was when I started to lose hope."

"You have the rest of your life to carve more – and there will be dozens of them, Jack. Dozens and dozens. Our children will tease us terribly about them all and I'll complain about dusting them because there'll be so many."

"We'll have children?"

"Lots! They'll run us ragged and you'll have to become a very successful sculptor to feed them all."

"I'd better get busy then," Jack said.

"Very!"

"I'll start by carving another angel for you," he decided, looking brighter. "To replace the one I lost."

"Maybe another soldier found her, and she's keeping *him* safe?" Caro suggested.

"I like that idea," Jack said linking hands with her. Their fingers wove together in the old and familiar way. "It feels as though she has a whole new story, a little like us. Caro, if your father's willing, let's be married as soon as I'm home. I don't want to wait any longer. Do you?"

"Not a second longer," said Caro firmly. "And don't worry about Papa. He'll be willing to give his consent."

Jack laughed. "Then I'd best pack my bag and tell the nurses I'm discharging myself. When's the next train to Cornwall?"

"This afternoon! Can you really leave?"

"Of course," said Jack. "They'll be glad to see the back of me moping about. Besides, I need to be back in Cornwall. I have a feeling I'll start working again once I'm home, you wait and see! I'll make a big success of myself. I'll build us a beautiful house overlooking the sea where I can hear the waves breaking and where all our children can run wild and drive you to distraction."

"Sea Angel," said Caro softly. She could see their house already and the happy life they would lead there and her arms were bobbled with goose bumps. It seemed to her as though this was a premonition.

"Sea Angel?" Jack echoed.

"The house we'll build. That's its name," she said.

"Sea Angel. I like that, and why not? I'm sure we have an angel looking after us."

"More than one," said Caro, and as they kissed again she had the strangest conviction that Jack's lost angel was still looking out for them, wherever she was and whoever was taking care of her now. Perhaps she always would?

"We're going home." Jack's hands rose to cup her cheek and Caro's happy tears ran through his fingers. His fingertips caressed her mouth and swept along the tilt of her nose, fluttering across her eyelids and whispering over the fine bones and planes of her face. "Our future will be wonderful. I don't need eyes to see that, for your face is etched on my heart and I see you still, Caro. You'll always be young and beautiful to me, and I'll spend the rest of my life loving you. Everything I create will always be for you and because of you. Everything. We have the rest of our lives to work out how, but for now it's enough to be with you. I want nothing more than that."

And Caro knew then that Jack's injury was not the end of his art but the very beginning. They would go home to Cornwall, be married and, as in all good fairy stories, they would live happily ever. Decades of Christmas angels, and a long and happy life together, lay ahead.

And today was just the beginning.

12

The present
December
Cornwall

Ellen

THE WINDOWS of the small teashop were fogged with heat from warm bodies and the steam hissing from the coffee maker. Perched on the side of the quay, and with a listing floor and a ceiling sliced by dark beams, it was the perfect place to sit in the window seat and watch the rolling waves beyond the harbour. Could this building have once been Jack's workshop? Little more than a shed tucked behind the fish market, it seemed a likely location.

"Anything?" she asked Anna who was busily scrolling through the internet.

Anna placed her phone down on the table and reached for her coffee.

"Not loads. Jack was big in the thirties but he fell out of fashion for decades. His first big piece was sold in 1923, and guess what it was?"

Ellen's hand stole to the angel in her pocket. "An angel by any chance?"

"Yep. It's in the Getty. Look."

Anna scooted the phone across the table, her hand shading it in order to prevent the reflected fairy lights obscuring the screen, and Ellen saw a huge angel, the big sister of the one nestling in her pocket but carved from marble and with broken soldiers crumpled at the hem of its robe. Some were on crutches and a few had missing limbs while others were bent double, cupping their spilled innards, and one raised sightless eyes to the angel's face. It was the most powerful and brutal piece of art she had ever seen.

"It sold in 2013 for $2.1 million," said Anna, taking her phone back and scrolling through the Wiki page. "It was purchased from a private collector in New York, not the Tregennas. It was a commission for an Italian count in the twenties."

"My goodness," said Ellen. Her head was spinning. Jack's work was worth millions today? That was ... incredible.

Anna's thumb continued swiping the screen. "Lots here about modernism blah blah and some stuff about later work. Seems Jack was in demand in the thirties and then fell out of fashion after the Second World War. He's collectable again now, though, and prices are rising, especially the early stuff ... Oh!"

Ellen pushed her coffee aside and leaned forward. "What?"

Anna's eyes were wide. "This. It's in the Guggenheim."

She turned the phone again. This time the screen was dark with the patina of aged wood, and looking closely Ellen saw carved angels arranged in a display case. She felt ridiculously moved to see that Jack had kept his promise and carved Caro an angel every Christmas for the rest of their lives together. They must have had a long and happy life.

"Yours must be worth a bomb," said Anna. "Don't lose it!"

Ellen's hand closed around the angel.

"She's safe with me."

"Art aside, the house that Bev mentioned, Sea Angel, is on Rightmove at just under £400,000 in case you're interested. It's got" – Anna made quotation marks in the air with her fingers – "*rare potential to be a stunning coastal residence and has been in the same family for over eighty years.* Maybe we should arrange a viewing?"

Ellen laughed out loud at the idea. "Blimey. Have your wages have gone up suddenly?"

"Not to buy, Els! Just for a nose around. Wouldn't you like to see where Jack and Caro ended up?" Anna was already reaching for her phone. "We'll give the agents a bell and scoot up."

"No we won't," said Ellen firmly. Experience had taught her it was best to rein her friend in sooner rather than later. "We're not stalkers. We'll walk up after breakfast and see it then. Maybe somebody will be about."

"Spoilsport," grumbled Anna.

"Guilty as charged," agreed Ellen.

"One bacon sandwich and one full English." A woman in a frilly pinny and mob cap, incongruous with tight leather-look leggings and hair the colour of Pepto-Bismol, set plates down on the table with a clatter. A tsunami of baked beans surged onto the placemat, and coffee sloshed in the mugs like the contents of a cruise ship pool in high seas.

"Any sauce?" she asked.

"Tomato, please," Anna said. "And some napkins if you have any."

The waitress sighed gustily, as though she'd been asked to embark on a quest for the Holy Grail. She returned with a squeezy ketchup bottle and a wodge of paper towels which she slammed onto the table in a begrudging fashion.

"Anything else?" she asked, crossing her arms as though daring them to say yes. A tattooed baby gurned from her bicep in an oddly menacing way. Ellen decided she didn't want brown sauce after all and opened her mouth to say they had everything they needed, but Anna was already asking questions.

"Actually, there is. Do you know anything about Sea Angel?"

The waitress eyed her suspiciously. "Come to look at it, have you?"

"In a way," said Anna. "We're interested in John Tregenna. The sculptor. Didn't he live there at one point?"

"Yeah, years ago. I think he built it. People sometimes come to see the stuff in the church that he did. He's buried there too, and arty types like to see the grave. They don't spend as much as the bucket and spade emmets. Emmets are holidaymakers," she explained when the girls looked puzzled. "Blooming emmets. That's what we call tourists round here."

"Good to know we're blooming emmets, right, Els?" said Anna.

But Ellen wasn't listening. She was thinking about Jack

sleeping in the peaceful churchyard, with his bones beneath the Cornish earth and his beloved Caro resting by his side. She'd been feet away from their resting place, and this idea was odd because to her they were still young people in love and with the whole world ahead of them. She felt as though she knew them and that she had always been meant to come to this place. It made no sense and yet it was the most right she thought she had ever felt, as though she had always been meant to be here today, sitting in this steamed-up teashop watching the wintry sea foam against the harbour wall and hopeful sunlight blanket stitch the edges of dove-grey clouds. There was a pattern she was woven into, and one by one the threads were drawing her closer to something, stitching her in until the design would finally be complete.

It was all to do with the lost angel and Granny Clara. Ellen was certain of it.

"Who lives at the house now?" she asked.

"Joss Tregenna," said the waitress. "Or he does until it sells, and then that'll be another local family gone."

"Jack's son?" Ellen pictured an elderly man with Jack's mop of hair now white as hoar frost and with Caro's sweet smile.

"No – grandson, I think. His father, Jolyon, married late. Took everyone by surprise because Mum said they all thought he was gay. Always with boats and fishermen and flouncing about painting. Just goes to show, doesn't it?"

Anna looked as though she was about to say something cutting, so Ellen said quickly, "The Tregennas still live there?"

"Yes, Joss and his mum, Cécile. She's not well at all. It's a terrible thing, cancer, isn't it?"

Anna and Ellen agreed that it was. The memory of caring for Clara in the final months, a memory that would retreat like the tide and come roaring back in like a rip, threatened to rise again and suck her under. She closed her fingers on the angel and held her tightly until the wash of loss retreated.

"Jolyon died last year," the waitress was saying conversationally. "He needed nursing care for the last few years and Cécile mortgaged the place to foot the bills for a nursing home. That's why the place is for sale. Care isn't cheap, is it?"

"No," said Ellen, remembering the astronomical fees when Clara was ill. Her heart went out to the unknown Joss Tregenna and his poorly mother, mired in paperwork and weighed down by exhaustion and sadness and the gruelling financial demands. "It really isn't."

The sympathy in her voice softened the waitress, who leaned forward and lowered her voice.

"Between you and me, they've not got a pot to piss in. All the money's long gone. They *need* to sell."

"What about the sculptures? I read that a Tregenna can fetch lots of money." Anna and Ellen exchanged glances, both thinking of the rare piece nestling in her pocket. "One of those would surely pay a lot of bills?"

"Wouldn't that be the dream? I imagine Jolyon sold what was left years ago to keep the place going. My mum said he was always abroad painting. That was where he met his wife. It was quite a scandal in these parts, what with him being in his sixties and her half his age and a foreigner!"

"Good for him," grinned Anna. "Hope for us yet, Els!"

Ellen laughed. "Maybe."

The waitress shook her head. "It's Joss I feel sorry for. It's his home. He paints up in the attic."

"He's an artist like Jack!" exclaimed Ellen.

How wonderful that Jack's talent had lived on in his son and his grandson. His legacy was far more than his art. It made her think about the invisible links that join the past and present, that join those long gone, whose names are forgotten, with those who are still alive. She knew that her own nose was Clara's and her wild hair came from her father's family, but the love of books, her amber eyes and the J-shaped mole on her thigh were mysteries. Who had borne these before? And what else had she inherited from these unknown ancestors?

"Some artist," sniffed the waitress. "Lots of splats is what it looks like. My five-year-old granddaughter could do better. If you ask me, being an artist's just a good excuse not to have a proper job."

"We've just met Cornwall's premier art critic," giggled Anna once the waitress was out of earshot. "Lord, I hope she never goes near the Tate Modern. Imagine what she'd make of unmade beds and cows in formaldehyde."

Ellen peeled open her sandwich, pulling the fat and rind away absently and flattening the soft white bread with the heel of her hand.

"It feels odd to hear all that about Jack and Caro's family but not know what happened to them both during the years between. It's like reading the beginning and ending of a book and missing all the chapters in the middle."

"We know Jack did well to have built that house, and we know that they had children," Anna pointed out through a mouthful of fried bread. "Maybe the middle bit wasn't very exciting? They had a happy life and a happy ending."

But as she watched the fishing boats tug at their moorings, Ellen thought that if the last member of Jack and Caro's family was about to lose the family home, the ending of their story seemed far from happy.

Unless, of course, this wasn't the end? What if this was

just a *part* of the story? What if the lost angel was still watching over the Tregennas? What if her work was not yet finished, and Heinrich and his family had been safeguarding her until the right moment?

Maybe the lost angel's work was only just beginning?

13

The Present
December
Cornwall

Ellen

ONCE BREAKFAST WAS OVER and they had drunk enough coffee to keep at bay the exhaustion from the long night drive to Cornwall, Ellen and Anna strolled through the village and explored the narrow streets, passing cottages Jack and Caro must have known and which, apart from sage paint and windows hung with Cath Kidston curtains, had changed little over the past century.

Eventually they left the village and began to climb the coast path to Sea Angel. It was a large and elegant house set high on the headland and accessible only by foot. Huge windows overlooked the rolling waves to make the most of the sea views and drench the rooms in light. A wrought-iron balcony wrapped around the first floor, inviting the outside and the inside to liaise, hinting at romantic evenings spent watching the last rays of the sun gilding the sea or breakfasts listening to seabirds. It was the perfect place for an artist to live, and Ellen imagined the older Jack ensconced in his attic studio where he would produce the work that would make his name and fortune. How heart-breaking to think that he would never have seen the view from the house.

"Slow down! I need to stop and catch my breath," puffed Anna. "This is way too steep for me. How does anyone get the shopping up?"

"Does it matter when it's so beautiful?" Ellen asked, already falling for the romance of the place. In her mind's eye she saw Caro walking back from the village, white skirts billowing in the salty wind like a full sail and Bramble dancing at her heels. She would wave at Jack high up in his attic studio even though he couldn't see her, and call out to him as she walked into the vaulted hallway, her heart swelling with happiness. Maybe there was a child, too, with wildflowers clutched in plump and sticky hands. Flowers for Daddy that he could smell even if he couldn't see them.

Her phone buzzed in her pocket. *Mum Mobile.*

"Take it. Please! Let me recover," begged Anna, clutching her side.

Laughing, Ellen answered the call.

"You sound as though you're having fun," said her mother.

"Yes, we are." It was true, Ellen realised with surprise. It was the first time in ages she hadn't felt the clawing sensation whenever she thought about Clara; instead she'd been filled with excitement about this unexpected quest, and the story of Jack and Caro, linked somehow to her own family, had soothed the sting of her grandmother's loss because she saw now that people were never really gone, were they? Not when others remembered them and spoke their names with love. Clara wasn't gone far away; she was just out of sight, sipping a Dubonnet with Grandpa Harry and squabbling over who watched what on the telly. She couldn't imagine Love Island would have been quite his thing.

"I'm glad, darling." Her mother sounded relieved, and Ellen realised then that her own sadness had added to her mother's burden of grief. How hard it was to be a parent. The pain and suffering of your children must cut even deeper than your own.

"Now, I'm about to dive into the Underground so before I lose signal I want to tell you that I called Sabine in Munich about that angel you found. I told you about her, remember?"

Ellen didn't remember. She'd never had that much interest in family history before. From now on, though, she'd find out all she could, she promised herself. She would uncover all the stories, however seemingly banal and trivial, and she'd make sure they were safeguarded and not forgotten.

"Did Sabine know anything more about where it came from?" Ellen asked.

"She did know a bit more, but she's very old and muddled these days and her English isn't very good. Anyway, she was told that my grandpa had found a wooden angel in No Man's Land on Christmas Day – the famous one in 1914 when the two sides had a truce. He'd been talking to a young man who he thought had dropped it."

"Jack Tregenna," Ellen breathed. She was hardly able to believe what she was hearing. Her great-grandfather had met and spoken to Jack on that long-ago Christmas morning when the fighting was paused so that men could celebrate and be at peace. How incredible to discover that her great-grandfather had witnessed an event which had assumed an almost mythological status.

"Who?" Maggie was confused.

"The man who carved the angel." Ellen was struggling to keep the note of impatience from her voice. "So Heinrich didn't steal it? You're sure he found it?"

"Of *course* he didn't steal it!" huffed Maggie, outraged. "My grandfather was a gentle soul, and to be honest I've no idea how he coped with warfare. He was normally to be found reading or tending his vegetables, or at least from what I remember of him. Sabine thinks he was hoping to return it when the war was over – but finding an English boy called Jack in the 1920s? Needles and haystacks spring to mind. She thought he'd had to give up. You know how many lads died, love. It was a hopeless search."

"If only he'd thought to take off the hessian robe," said Ellen sadly. "Then he could have returned it in person."

She looked up at Sea Angel and imagined Great-grandfather Heinrich standing right where she was now and staring up at the imposing house. His hand would close on the angel just as hers did now, then he would square his shoulders and press on. Spare and straight-backed and sporting old-fashioned wire-framed spectacles, he would have been out of place amongst fisherfolk, but she felt sure that had he been able to meet Jack Tregenna once more they would have become firm friends. It was oddly circular that she was here today, a fish out of water too, but about to meet a man without whose family her own would have never existed.

"Perhaps he didn't feel he should meddle with what wasn't his?" offered her mother. "We'll never know now. But there's more. Let me tell you quickly, before I have to dash off.

I'm meeting Dan for lunch. You know how he hates people being late."

Ellen did. Her brother was terribly impatient. He always had been, and she wondered where this trait came from. Was it unique to Dan, or an echo of a long-forgotten family member? All these echoes of the past were just a whisper away from the present, it seemed.

"Anyway, Sabine said the story is that my grandfather had that wooden angel tucked into his breast pocket when he and his men were attacked. There was hand-to-hand combat and he was in the thick of it. Apparently it stopped the tip of a bayonet entering his chest. That was when he lost his arm, but without that angel it would have been a lot worse."

"The angel's got a deep cut in her trunk," Ellen said quietly. She had watched over Heinrich too – of course she had. Angels didn't take sides.

"There you go then," said her mother briskly. "My goodness, to think that if it wasn't for that funny little carving Granny Clara wouldn't have been born, would she? And then neither you nor I would be here, would we?"

"No," Ellen agreed. It was a lot to take in.

"I feel bad about painting her now! Seems to me that our family owes her quite a lot," Maggie concluded.

They certainly did, and now it was time to return the favour. Ellen knew exactly what she was going to do with the angel. It was so obvious. Maybe it had been destined to happen this way?

"Come on," she said to Anna, after filling her in on Sabine's history. "Let's see if anyone's in."

Even though her calves burned from the climb Ellen was fired up with excitement and sprinted up the last of the incline which led to the gate. If only Clara had still been alive!

She knew her grandmother would have enjoyed this adventure so much, and would have loved to know her treasured angel's secrets. What would she had thought if she'd known it had been crafted by a renowned sculptor? Somehow, Ellen didn't think this would have mattered a jot to her grandmother; Clara loved it for what it meant, and not for what it was worth.

Sea Angel announced a weathered sign on a once beautiful gate, now salt-nibbled and peeling paint like sunburned skin, and *For Sale!* declared the board hammered into the frosty ground beside it. Close up, the house, although beautiful, was neglected, the windows salt-crusted and cracked in places, and the stonework in need of pointing. The beautiful iron balcony, so impressive from below, was coming away from the wall, and the paved path leading to a large oak door had risen with roots. Lichen had velveted the stone steps which rose up to the slab of the studded front door. A once grand porch was flanked by huge sash windows which would flood the ground floor with light, and stone urns blackened with moss rested on each side of it, filled with the sad remains of summer flowers. Once they must have brimmed with lavender and swayed with the drunken buzzing of bees, once long ago when this place was in its prime. Even the gnarled wisteria snaking its way over the windows, a plant which would drip with rich purple blooms in summer, seemed a skeleton of its old self.

The Tregennas had fallen on hard times and although Sea Angel was the perfect project for somebody wealthy and with the budget to throw at it, Ellen's heart was heavy to that think Jack and Caro's home was slipping away from the family they had built it for.

"See if anyone's in?" called Anna, blowing on her hands

and shivering in her fashionable but thin jacket. “I’m freezing.”

Ellen lifted the heavy brass door knocker, jumping at the loudness of the hammering, but there was no shuffle of footsteps followed by the slow opening of the door. She waited for a few moments before knocking once again, but still the only answer was the lonely calling of the gulls.

“It doesn’t look like it,” she said, stepping back and cricking her neck to peer upwards and the dark windows.

“Let’s try again later.” Anna said, keen to exchange the biting wind for warmth. She checked her watch. “Let’s check into the B & B, then then head into Penhayes to do some Christmas shopping. Apparently there are some really high-end shops, and a celebrity chef has a café. Gordon Ramsay? Rick Stein? Somebody like that, anyway. We can treat ourselves to lunch.”

Ellen nodded, but she felt deflated. She’d been so sure she was meant to be here, and that Clara was watching from somewhere not so very far away and urging her on, that to meet a dead end was crushing. Had she been deluding herself and looking for signs where there were none? She touched the angel again, willing it to work a little miracle, but the studded door remained firmly closed. No curtains twitched as an elderly inhabitant peeped out to see who was knocking on his door, and no kindly old man let them in. She turned away, resigned to abandoning the whole idea as a wild goose chase.

“You go back and check us in. I’d like to walk a bit further along the cliff path,” she said.

Anna, whose nose was going blue, didn’t need telling twice. Agreeing they would meet at the guest house in an hour’s time, Anna scurried away down the path while Ellen paused, looking up at the house, crumbling and ivy-covered, but no less beautiful with its windows golden in the pale winter sunshine.

"Hello, there! Can I help you at all?"

A man appeared at the side of the house, shielding his eyes against the sun as he regarded at her in a rather confused fashion. In the winter sunlight his thatch of hair, gold shot through with silver threads, became a nimbus and lent him an angelic appearance. As he squinted against the glare, green eyes starred with laughter lines peered at Ellen against the brightness and he smiled at her quizzically.

"Are you collecting for charity? Christ! You're not a high court bailiff are you? I ought to tell you that the front door hasn't opened for about a decade, the bolts have probably seized, and you couldn't come in even if you tried. And if you did get in through the back door because I'd left it open, there's absolutely nothing of any value here unless you want a painting. Actually I've got loads of those. Take two! Maybe they could have value as investments for the future?"

He looked so pleased by this idea that Ellen thought he was about to rush off and fetch her one.

"I'm not collecting for charity and I'm definitely not a bailiff," she said quickly.

"Phew!" said the man. "I think I watched far too much 'Can't Pay? We Take It Away!' during lockdown, but Mum's useless at paying bills on time so you never quite know. She usually hides the brown envelopes in a teapot or under the sink and hopes that out of sight is out of mind – which doesn't really work so well."

Ellen laughed. "I've tried that myself and it doesn't work at all!"

"No," he agreed, waving a paintbrush-clutching hand at

the For Sale sign. "Have you come for a viewing? Only nobody said, and I'm right in the middle of something."

Looking at him more closely as he stepped towards her, Ellen saw that he was wearing a fisherman's smock, once ocean blue but now daubed in a rainbow of paint smears. His faded jeans were speckled with ochre and violet and woodland green, and even his left cheekbone bore a smudge of vermilion. His feet were bare and tanned, as though he had been in such a hurry to answer the door he hadn't stopped to shove them into shoes.

"I was working in my studio. It's in the attic and I dashed right down when I heard you at the door," he explained, catching her curious glance. "I'm a mess. Sorry. We don't have many visitors this far up the hill."

"You're Joss Tregenna," Ellen said slowly. Of course he was! Even if he hadn't been painting she would have known him. She recognised that smile and the pure angles of his face. Rather than smooth wood, Joss Tregenna's cheeks might be peppered with gold and silver stubble and rough to touch, but she could feel every curve beneath her fingertips right now as she brushed the countenance of the lost angel. She had seen his smile on the lips of the angels gracing the rood screen in the church and it was replicated on the mouth of the sculpture residing in a private collection across the Atlantic. Ellen would have known that smile anywhere, for it was the same smile Jack Tregenna had fallen in love with over one hundred years ago, and the one he'd carved for the rest of his lifetime. Even when he had lost his sight Jack Tregenna saw that smile and held it close to his heart, for it was Caroline Sweethouse's smile and it lived on in their grandson.

Ellen knew she was staring but she couldn't help herself. "I'm Ellen Shaw," she said.

"Sorry, do I know you from somewhere?" Joss stepped towards her, looking puzzled. He tucked the paintbrush behind his ear and wiped his hand on his jeans before holding it out. "I feel sure I know you. Have we met before?"

Ellen shook her head. "We haven't met," she said, although it felt as though she knew the man intimately, knew how the hair curled in the nape of his neck and how the sweep of dark lashes fanned his cheeks when his eyes were closed. She knew that his golden hair was Caro's and the deep green eyes were Jack's and that the dimple which starred his left cheek was his alone. It was as though the angel nestled in her pocket had come to life.

His smile caught and now she was smiling too. Shaking Joss's hand, warm and strong as it clasped hers, felt like returning to the safe harbour of a long-lost and once-cherished friendship. Did Heinrich and Jack's descendants' clasped hands retain some memory of that long-ago handshake on No Man's Land? Or was this something more?

"You'll know him when you find him, love, because it feels like coming home. Never settle for less than that." Clara's words seemed to whisper on the wind and cry with the gulls. The skin at the nape of Ellen's neck tingled.

"So what brings you here, Ellen Shaw?" Joss Tregenna asked.

Ellen was poised to tell him about her the lost angel and how the carving was connected to his own family when a small spaniel shot around the corner of the house and bounded towards her barking loudly and with its plumed tail wagging and long ears flapping in comic-book fashion. For a moment

Ellen thought she had travelled back in time and she glanced at the terrace expecting to see Caro running after it, frantically calling for the naughty animal to come back. Bramble?

Joss caught the dog's collar with practised ease. "No jumping!" he scolded. "Don't worry, he's friendly."

Ellen bent down and stroked the silky head while the dog licked her hand and tried his hardest to jump up.

"Down, Bramble," said Joss, tugging him back. "Sorry! He's a law unto himself."

"He's called Bramble too?"

"You've been here before then? I thought I recognised you."

"No."

Joss looked confused. "But you must have been to the village then? Everyone here knows it's our family's tradition to have a spaniel called Bramble. Very unimaginative, I know, but my father said his mother insisted on it. The first Bramble was very badly behaved too, and had a habit of running away. It's apparently how my grandparents met."

"He ran away down the cliff path," Ellen said quietly, "and Jack caught him. It was love at first sight for them both."

Joss straightened up, puzzled. "Yes! – but how do you know all that?"

Ellen wanted to tell him but felt nervous. Would he think she was crazy? A stalker? Or an angel thief?

"Ellen?" Joss said, softly. He was closer now and although they weren't touching, the small space between them felt charged with a static she knew he could feel too. "How do you know that?"

She looked out over the grey sea and gilt-edged clouds, searching for the right words. She poised on the edge of something that would change both their futures. She could turn away right now, join Anna at the B & B and return to the village with the angel still in her pocket. It was worth a fortune and it was hers. She could sell it and enjoy the proceeds.

Or she could do what she knew was right.

"You know what to do," she heard Clara say. "Trust your instincts, my love, for they're never wrong."

"It's a long story," she said, turning to Joss. "It starts with my great-grandfather and the First World War."

"I'm intrigued. My grandfather fought in the trenches. I never met him, but my dad said he never got over it. Who could? The horrors they witnessed must have haunted those who came home."

Ellen reached into her pocket where the angel was waiting. She had been waiting patiently for over one hundred years for this moment, and very soon would be with her own family.

"I think my great-grandfather met your grandfather in France," she said.

He nodded. "It's possible, I guess. Did they serve together?"

"That's not how they met. They fought on opposite sides. My great-grandfather was German, you see, but he met your grandfather and found this."

She slipped the carved angel from her pocket and held it out to him.

"The Lost Angel!" Joss looked floored.

"You know about her?"

"Of course I do. She's a family legend. My grandfather carved her for my grandmother. He made one for her every Christmas, but this one was precious because he'd made her at the Front. He lost her in the trenches and apparently he never forgot it. He'd believed she was his guardian angel, and maybe he was right because just after that he was badly injured and lost his sight."

"My great-grandfather found her," Ellen explained. "He cherished her by all accounts, because she saved his life by taking a blow that would have killed him."

Joss whistled. "A guardian angel for him too, then. But how did you find out she was my grandfather's? Did you see the Kit Rivers exhibition? Kit was my grandfather's commanding officer, but I didn't think my grandfather's mentioned in it."

Ellen smiled. "It's a long story."

"Then I think you'd better come inside and tell it," Joss Tregenna said.

14

The present
Cornwall
Ellen

Joss showed Ellen around the side of the house and through the back door.

"Sorry about the mess," he said as they hopscotched over abandoned shoes and toppled wellingtons strewn throughout a boot room lined so deeply with coats Ellen thought if she burrowed deep enough she would find one of Caro's – or else arrive in Narnia!

"It reminds me of the porch at my grandmother's. I think she kept every coat and pair of boots she ever owned," she said.

She waited for the little claw of sadness which always came whenever she thought of Granny Clara but it didn't arrive. Instead she felt a warm fondness for her grandmother's hoarding ways.

"I keep meaning to tidy up – the estate agent's always nagging me to make it presentable – but I'm putting it off," he said, picking up a lone croc and placing it in a rack beside its twin. "You can probably see why. It's like an excavation. We've lived here for donkeys' years."

Ellen wasn't sure how to reply. Joss seemed comfortable talking about Sea Angel being for sale but from what Bev the Rev and the waitress in the coffee shop had said, she suspected that the sale was a forced one.

"I think it's great. A real family home."

"It's certainly that. My grandfather had it built in the thirties. He'd made a bit of name for himself as a sculptor and sold a couple of pieces. They loved it here." Sadness flittered over his face. "We all do, but things change, don't they?"

"I guess."

There was a pause and then, as though he had been weighing up how much to say, Joss shrugged ruefully. "The bottom line is Dad needed full-time care for the last few years of his life. He had Parkinson's and we couldn't manage, no matter how much we wanted to. Mum tried, but it was so hard – and she isn't well, either." He swallowed, struggling to keep his emotion in check.

"I'm so sorry," Ellen said.

"Thanks, but that's life I suppose. Denybole Hall had the care Dad needed and it was best for him, but it left Mum and me rattling around here and with a few bills to cover."

Ellen imagined it had.

"Let's go and find Mum," Joss was saying. "She'll love to see the angel."

He stepped back from the door to let Ellen pass, his hand hovering over the small of her back and although there was no touch her pulse quickened. Flustered, she asked him about Jack and Caro and how they had come by the house, and Joss was happy to tell her.

"My grandfather came home a wounded hero," he said as they passed along a narrow corridor. "There were lots of men like him, I believe, and he could have become bitter about losing his sight but that wasn't in his nature. He was deeply in love with my grandmother. They were blissfully happy by all accounts and so grateful he came home."

"My great-grandparents were the same," Ellen recalled. Heinrich and Heidi Schneider had been devoted, according to Granny Clara, just as she and Grandpa Harry had been. It was hard sometimes not to be a little jealous.

"They were lucky too, and I bet they knew it," Joss said. "So many of their generation didn't make it home. Anyway, my grandfather returned to carpentry, which can't have been easy without his sight, but when my grandmother was twenty-one she inherited a large amount of money and they travelled through the continent. They went to France and Italy and even down to Spain and Morocco. It was like a giant gap year!"

All the places they had dreamed of, Ellen recalled, and her vision blurred. They had done it.

"That was when they had a little bit of luck," Joss continued. "The story goes that they were in Florence and met a wealthy Italian who was really taken with my grandfather. He became his patron, and the rest, as they say, is history. After several years living in Italy and saving hard they returned to Cornwall and later on they built this place and lived here for the rest of their lives."

It was wonderful to know Jack and Caro had their happy

ever after, and Ellen felt something in her heart lighten. Maybe she could believe in love after all? Clara had always told her that love was waiting to be found. She'd sent an angel. Did this mean that love was next?

As they walked through the house Joss explained how Caro had planted the jasmine which scrambled across the walls so Jack could smell the heady scent when he sat in the garden or opened the windows in his studio, and he pointed out the rough angels his grandfather had etched into many places around the house.

"There's one in the laundry room and another behind the bookcase in the study," he said. "I think there's one in the loo and the pantry. It was a bit of a love code between them. Beats graffiti!"

She laughed. "Far more romantic!"

As she followed Joss through a corridor and into a hall, Ellen was struck by how light and welcoming the place was as it opened up. Gone was the wooden panelling of the corridor, and in its place white walls bouncing liquid light from a cupola opening above their heads like a glass umbrella. Even on a grey wintry day the intense light was pure and created the perfect foil for six enormous canvases depicting sailing boats.

"My father painted those," Joss said, seeing her admiring them.

"They're stunning."

He looked pleased by her praise. "Thanks. I think so too. He was enormously talented. I find them totally compelling and I often find I've lost hours simply staring at them."

"He was an artist too?"

"He was, but only as a hobby. Pa loved painting boats,

because he worked with them. He ran a chandlery in Penhayes for donkeys' years until ..." He paused and visibly collected himself. "Well, until he couldn't. Lord knows where we'll put these paintings when we move. They fit this place. We all do. It's home."

The sadness in what remained unsaid was palpable and the skin around his mouth tautened. Ellen had caught a glimpse of the strain Joss Tregenna was under, and her heart twisted for him.

"I love the light," she offered, and he grasped the change of topic gratefully.

"It's amazing, isn't it? My grandmother had the cupola put in for my grandfather. He was blind, but they discovered he could distinguish between light and darkness, and he loved the sunshine. I believe they had a few of his pieces displayed here once."

Looking a little more closely Ellen realised there were alcoves set back from the walls. Some were filled with books. Others were crammed with a jumble of hats and scarves and dog leads. A stuffed bear wearing a Santa hat sat in another. The effect was homely and welcoming, she thought, because this was not a museum or gallery but a much-loved family home. A woodburner glowed in the large fireplace and the air was rich with the smell of baking bread and something meaty, a hearty casserole perhaps bubbling away on the Aga, or soup? A large clock tick-tocked away the minutes from the mantel, its round face reflected in a large age-spotted mirror hanging on the opposite wall, to capture more light and repeat the paintings of boats and water into a ripple of infinity.

"Anyway, come and find Mum. She'll love to hear all

about this," Joss said, turning away and ushering her along another corridor. This one led to the kitchen where battered copper pans and tomato-soup-orange Le Creuset pots hung precariously from thick beams, each festooned in dried herbs and loops of fairy lights. Just as Ellen had imagined there was a large Aga, but rather than a pot of soup on the hotplate there was a wok piled with cushions and inhabited by an enormous ginger cat. A huge Welsh dresser was at the far end of the room, displaying blue and white Cornish ware plates which peeked out shyly from behind Christmas cards like geishas behind fans. The walls were painted a sunny yellow and were adorned with big splashy canvases, as bright and as cheerful as a summer's day, depicting scenes of vivid blue seas, higgledy-piggledy rooftops and swooping orange-footed gulls. They were vibrant and fresh and fun.

"Oh! I love those!" cried Ellen.

"They're mine," Joss said shyly.

"They're great. They make me feel it's summer," she said. "I can hear the gulls and feel the sunshine just looking at them. Honestly, I love them."

He blushed. "Thanks. They're not as intricate as Pa's oils, and I can't lay claim to anything like my grandfather's talent, but I'm quite pleased with how they turned out."

"My son is far too modest. I don't suppose he's mentioned he was featured last year in the Royal Academy's summer exhibition?"

A slender woman, her silver hair drawn up into a ballerina bun, was seated at the kitchen table writing Christmas cards. Although in her late seventies, and so thin the heavy silver rings on her fingers weighed her hands down, her dark eyes were as bright and as lively as Mrs Tiggywinkle's, and the lightly accented voice was youthful.

"Mum, don't," groaned Joss.

"But it is true, *chérie*."

"This is my mum and greatest fan, Cécile Tregenna," he said with an eye roll. "Mum, this is Ellen Shaw."

Cécile held out a hand, which Ellen shook tentatively, because Cécile's bones were as light as air and her skin tissue-paper thin, and Ellen felt as though she could blow away.

"Nice to meet you," said Ellen.

Cécile nodded, regarding her with mingled curiosity and suspicion. "*Enchantée*. Do you paint, Ellen? Is this why you're interested in this house? You're an artist, *non*? You wish to use the studio?"

"Oh no! I'm not viewing the house!" Ellen glanced at Joss who nodded encouragingly. She took a breath, and said, "I'm here about this."

She placed the angel on the red and white polka-dot oilcloth which covered the kitchen table and Cécile gasped. Her hand rose to her throat.

"*Mon dieu*! I don't believe it! The Lost Angel!" She turned the angel around in her hands.

Ellen gently took the angel from Cècile, springing open the secret compartment with ease. "There's a secret place, see? Jack hid a letter in it."

Cècile gasped. Her hand fluttered to her throat.

"My goodness," said Joss.

"I found this by chance when I was cleaning her up, and I read the letter. That's how I managed to trace you. I hope that's all right?" said Ellen.

Cécile dabbed her eyes with her sleeve. "But of course! We are just so happy you chose to let us know she's safe. How did you come by this angel when she was lost so long ago?"

"My great-grandfather, Heinrich, found her. Wrong side, I guess, but he'd met Jack earlier on and liked him."

"Heinrich?" Cécile reached across the table and clutched Ellen's arm. "Heinrich was your great-grandfather?"

"You've heard of him?"

"*Mais oui! Bien sur!*" Cécile turned to Joss, speaking rapidly in French and with wild gesticulations. Ellen, who could just about order a croque monsieur and find the way to the station, was utterly lost.

"Sorry, Mum always speaks French when she's excited," Joss said. "Mum, tell Ellen *slowly* and in English, what you just told me while I put the kettle on."

Cécile screwed up her nose in horror. "Coffee for me. Brewed properly and not out of a jar. You English – you have no idea!"

Joss rolled his eyes fondly. This was clearly a discussion they had regularly. While he ground beans and frothed milk, Cécile smoothed out Caro's letter with gentle fingers and kissed the angel's sweet face.

"She has your smile," she said to Joss. "Just like all the others. My father-in-law carved forty-eight, I believe. He and Caroline were together for a long time and they adored one another right until the very end."

"Do you have the angels here?" Ellen was hopeful, but Cécile looked sad.

"*Non*, they're long gone. They were bought by an American collector. My husband sold them before he met me. Poor Jolyon, he tried his best, but in the end he had no choice. He sold all of his father's work to make ends meet."

"That's so sad," Ellen said.

Cécile gave a gallic shrug. "It is what it is. I think Jack would have understood."

"Tell Ellen how you know her great-grandfather's name," Joss prompted, setting down coffee that was rich and thick and dark as night. He opened a cake tin crammed with mince pies, all dusted with sugar and shedding flakes of golden pastry. He offered one to Ellen and she took it, suddenly hungry and no longer feeling the need to avoid a festive speciality. The climb and the salty air and the excitement had given her an appetite and chased away the heavy sadness that had weighed her down for so long. She bit into it and tasted raisins and peel and Christmas, transported across the years to the child helping her grandmother to bake for the big night.

"Ah, but that's simple to explain," said Cécile. She waved away a mince pie, still caressing the angel incredulously. "My father-in-law, Jack, often spoke of the Christmas Day truce. He remembered it with mixed emotions, for it was wonderful on the one hand to see enemies become friends and to celebrate peace, yet it was also sad for him because he lost the angel and, shortly after, his sight. So many of his friends, too, died in the attack which blinded him. But he said he was impressed by a German soldier he had met on Christmas Day – Heinrich he was called, and he was a teacher. Jack always hoped he made it through."

"He did," Ellen said, "but only because of Jack or, more accurately, his lost angel. You see, Jack must have dropped her while he was playing football, because my grandfather found her on the ground."

"Go on," said Cécile, leaning forward.

Ellen sipped her coffee, and repeated more of the story that her cousin Sabine had told her mother.

"So Jack's lost angel saved my grandfather's life. If not for her, I wouldn't exist," Ellen finished. "None of my family would. We owe her, and Jack Tregenna, everything. Apparently Heinrich searched for Jack but never found him, but I know he treasured the angel. He knew Jack's work had saved his life."

"From war and death came friendship and a future," said Cécile approvingly. "I think my father-in-law would have liked that idea. May I have a little time to read the letter? I would dearly love to."

Ellen picked up the angel and her heart ached a little because she knew it was time to say farewell.

"You can have all the time in the world," she said. "She's yours. This is where she belongs."

Jack Tregenna had made this angel for his beloved Caro. The lost angel had watched over him faithfully before saving a man who should have been her creator's sworn enemy. The angel belonged to this man who bore her gentle smile and head of golden curls, and she was where she belonged.

As she caressed the sweet wooden face for the final time Ellen knew the angel had always been waiting for the right moment to return. The design had been woven over decades, but now the loom was stopped because the pattern was complete. Somewhere Granny Clara was nodding her approval and beaming and pointing at Joss as though he was one of the hunks lined up on Love Island: *Live a little.*

I will, Ellen promised her silently. *I will.*

She held the angel to Joss. "She belongs to you."

"Ellen, I can't." Joss was shocked. "She's very valuable."

"You must." Ellen was adamant. The angel would keep the last of the Tregennas safe and could save Sea Angel. She had only ever been on loan to the Schneiders, and it was time they repaid their debt.

"But she's been in your family for so long."

"Maybe, but she was made for Caro, and you're Caro's grandson. That means she's yours." She stared into his deep green eyes and thought of deep coves and emerald rock pools, and was shocked how much she longed to keep looking at him. Her mouth was dry and her heart raced. A single ray of sunshine slipped out from behind a cloud and turned his hair to gold, making the similarity between this man and the angel unmistakable.

I'll send your perfect match over. You see if I don't. Keep your eyes peeled for that sign! He'll be your angel.

Your angel ...

Here he is! Clara's delighted laughter couldn't have been louder if she had been in the room, and Ellen glanced over her shoulder expecting to see her grandmother smiling. But there was only the purring cat on his toasty perch and the gentle notes of carols floating from a radio.

"Ellen?" Joss said. "Is everything okay?"

Ellen looked back at Joss. "Yes it is," she said.

Joss smiled at her, a warm and sweet smile that made her breath catch, and now Ellen was Jack, standing on the beach watching the love of his life slither and slide down the path and straight into his heart. Like this one, theirs was a meeting neither had expected or sought, but it was one which had changed their lives for ever. Jack had known that Caro Sweethouse was the one.

How did you know? Ellen had often wondered. People said that you just did, which always seemed a weak answer – but now she understood that they were right. It was a feeling of certainty and peace. There was no need to question it, and Ellen knew beyond all doubt that she had always been meant to come to this place. This moment had been destined to happen from the second the angel had slipped from Jack's pocket and into the mire. Heinrich and Jack's chance meeting wasn't chance at all; it was part of something far bigger. Wars and kingdoms and politics came and went – but love and friendship and the memory of that long-ago Christmas truce?

These things lived on for ever.

"You must take the angel," she said softly. "It's what my grandmother would want."

Joss placed his hands over Ellen's, tenderly folding the angel and her fingers inside his own. His touch felt so familiar and so right, and she saw the same emotion mirrored in his wondering expression.

I know you, it said. *I'm sure I do.*

You do, hers replied. *You always have.*

"Are you sure?" Cécile said. "It's worth a lot of money, Ellen, and it's yours. We lost her years ago."

Ellen nodded. "She belongs to you, and it's the right thing. Please take her. She was never ours. We were only taking care of her for the Tregennas. I know my grandmother and her father would have said the same thing. Now let her take care of you. Jack would want that, wouldn't he?"

Joss Tregenna exhaled slowly. Ellen knew he understood that owning the angel would change everything for his family. Jack's angel truly was a guardian angel.

"Thank you," he said softly. "Thank you for coming here and for bringing her back. Thank you, Ellen."

And as his hands squeezed hers, Ellen saw the tug of attraction was reflected in Joss Tregenna's sea-green eyes and felt sure that wherever she was now, Granny Clara was smiling too – and so were Jack and Heinrich. Young again and free to be friends, they knew the angel was no longer lost and the families they had built were safe and loved. The warmth of Joss's hand on hers promised Ellen this was so, and she smiled at him, certain all was now exactly as it was meant to be.

Just like the lost angel, Ellen was home at last.

The End

EPILOGUE

Rare Tregenna piece to be auctioned at Broneways

An opportunity has arisen to purchase an early work by the twentieth-century Cornish sculptor John Tregenna. Believed to have been carved while Tregenna was serving on the Western Front in 1914, the Lost Angel is attracting international attention from both private collectors and galleries, for the piece is unique – not least because it dates from the period prior to Tregenna losing his sight.

LITTLE IS KNOWN about the sculptor himself, for Tregenna lived quietly in Cornwall and was devoted to his schoolmistress wife and son. He was born in Cornwall, the only son of a carpenter, and his work attracted critical acclaim in the nineteen-thirties; it is now increasingly sought after. Critics debate whether his assured style is a re-interpretation of Renaissance art or a unique style, but agree that his use of form is both innovative and distinctive. The angel is the second piece in a series Tregenna carved for his wife. The other pieces are in museums, including the Guggenheim, and private collections.

THE LOST ANGEL occupies a unique place in art history. Indeed its value lies in this as much as it does in the scarcity of Tregenna's work. The piece was missing until last year, when it came to light in the effects of a descendant of the German soldier who had found it during the famous Christmas Day truce of 1914. A letter written by Tregenna's wife accompanies the angel and enhances the story behind this find. Links to the First World War poet Kit Rivers and the Rosecraddick Set add value to the piece and have sparked great excitement among collectors. The Cornish Heritage Trust has expressed interest, as has the Tate Modern, and the Lost Angel is expected to create great excitement when it comes to auction next week.

EWAN HAWKE, Modern Art Expert at Broneways, says, "The rarity of Tregenna's work only adds to its desirability amongst art collectors. The story behind this piece is truly remarkable, and it is as much a historical artefact as it is a work of art. To be handling the sale of the Lost Angel is a privilege."

THE CURRENT OWNER of the Lost Angel is Joss Tregenna, the grandson of the sculptor. With the proceeds of the sale

Tregenna and his fiancée, who is by a quirk of fate a direct descendant of the German soldier who discovered the angel, intend to restore John Tregenna's home and open it to the public to celebrate his life and work.

THE GUIDE PRICE is £250,000.

THE DAILY RECORD
June 2022

THANK YOU

I really hope you have enjoyed reading this book. If you did, I would really appreciate a review on Amazon. It makes all the difference for an author and helps new readers discover and enjoy the book.

Amazon UK

Amazon.com

ABOUT THE AUTHOR

Ruth Saberton in her boat on the Fowey Estuary

Ruth Saberton is the bestselling author of *The Letter, Katy Carter Wants a Hero* and *Escape for the Summer*. She has also written upmarket commercial fiction under the pen names Jessica Fox, Georgie Carter and Holly Cavendish.

Born in London, Ruth now lives in beautiful Cornwall. She has travelled to many places, but nothing compares to the rugged beauty of the Cornish coast which never fails to provide her with inspiration for her writing. Ruth loves to chat with readers so please follow her author pages on Instagram and Facebook You can also follow her on Twitter.

Head over to Ruth's website for more information about her and her writing. You can also sign up for her newsletter where you'll receive updates on any new releases and other exciting items.

ALSO BY RUTH SABERTON

You might also enjoy my other books:

Oyster Shore

The Promise

The Last Card

The Letter

The Locket

The Island Legacy

Chances

Runaway Summer: Polwenna Bay 1

A Time for Living: Polwenna Bay 2

Winter Wishes: Polwenna Bay 3

Treasure of the Heart: Polwenna Bay 4

Recipe for Love: Polwenna Bay 5

Rhythm of the Tide: Polwenna Bay 6

Catching Hearts: Polwenna Bay 7

Christmas by Candlelight: Polwenna Bay 8

Magic in the Mist: Polwenna Bay novella

Cornwall for Christmas: Polwenna Bay novella

Escape for the Summer

Escape for Christmas

Hobb's Cottage

Weight Till Christmas

The Wedding Countdown

Dead Romantic

Katy Carter Wants a Hero

Katy Carter Keeps a Secret

Ellie Andrews Has Second Thoughts

Amber Scott is Starting Over

Pen Name Books

Writing as Jessica Fox

The One That Got Away

Eastern Promise

Hard to Get

Unlucky in Love

Always the Bride

Writing as Holly Cavendish

Looking for Fireworks

Writing as Georgie Carter

The Perfect Christmas

Printed in Great Britain
by Amazon

18313816R00112